MY BROTHER IS A SUPERHERO

DAVID SOLOMONS

MY BROTHER IS A SUPERHERO

DAVID SOLOMONS

VIKING
An Imprint of Penguin Group (USA)

VIKING
Published by the Penguin Group
Penguin Group (USA) LLC
375 Hudson Street
New York, New York 10014

USA ✽ Canada ✽ UK ✽ Ireland ✽ Australia ✽ New Zealand
India ✽ South Africa ✽ China

penguin.com
A Penguin Random House Company

First published in the United Kingdom by Nosy Crow, 2015
Published simultaneously in the United States of America by Viking,
an imprint of Penguin Young Readers Group, 2015

Copyright © 2015 by David Solomons

LIBRARY OF CONGRESS CATALOGING-IN-PUBLICATION DATA
Solomons, David, date–
My brother is a superhero / by David Solomons.
pages cm
Summary: When his older brother Zack is zapped by an alien and turned into a superhero,
eleven-year-old Luke, a hard-core fan of comics and superheroes, is understandably chagrined
until a plot to destroy the earth incapacitates Zack, and Luke, accompanied by Lara, the plucky
girl next door, must come to the rescue.
ISBN 978-0-451-47477-3
[1. Brothers—Fiction. 2. Superheroes—Fiction. 3. Cartoons and comics—Fiction.] I. Title.
PZ7.1.S67My 2015
[Fic]—dc23
2014030547

Printed in the USA

10   9   8   7   6   5   4   3   2   1

Designed by Eileen Savage
Set in Mendoza Roman Std

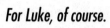

For Luke, of course.

MY BROTHER IS A SUPERHERO

THE [NOT] CHOSEN ONE

My brother is a superhero, and I could have been one too, except that I needed to go pee.

My name is Luke Parker. I'm eleven years old, and I live in a mild-mannered part of the city with my mom, dad, and big brother, Zack. He wasn't always a super-hero, but with a name like Zack you've got to wonder if my parents had a hunch that one day he'd end up wear-ing a mask and cape and saving orphans from burning buildings. I mean, come on! It's not a name; it's a sound effect. It's what you get in a comic when a superhero punches a supervillain. *Pow! Blam! Zack!*

It seems to me that in life you are faced with clear-cut moments when things could go one way or another. Vanilla or chocolate. Smooth or crunchy. Drop the water balloon on Dad's head or hold your fire. It's up to you which choice to make, and sometimes all it takes to change the way your whole life turns out are four little words.

"I need to pee."

It was the fateful evening. Zack and I had been in our tree house for about an hour, and I was bursting. I was reading an old issue of Teen Titans by flashlight, Zack was doing his math homework. He's always been a bit of a teacher's pet. Before he became Star Guy, at school he was star boy.

"Then go," he said, solving another quadratic equation with a flick of his pencil. "I'm not stopping you."

The truth was I didn't want to go down the rope ladder in the dark. It had been hard enough climbing up it in the first place. It's not that I'm out of shape or anything, but put it like this: you won't ever see me on an Olympic podium. I suffer from hay fever and have funny-shaped feet that mean I have to wear these things in my shoes called "orthotics." When Mom first told me I needed them, I was excited. I thought they sounded like supersoldier power armor, but when they finally arrived they turned out to be bendy, foot-shaped supports and not a cybernetic exoskeleton suit. That was a disappointing Thursday.

I hung my head out of the tree house door. "Maybe I could just pee from here?"

"Out! Get out of here, you disgusting child!"

Zack is only three years older than me, but when I've done something to annoy him he calls me a child. Of all the things I can't stand about my big brother, being called a child is number forty-seven. Not that I have a list.

OK. I do have a list.

Even before he became a superhero, the list was up to sixty-three. Now it's almost at a hundred. He is *very* irritating.

I climbed down the rope ladder and went into the house.

I peed.

When I returned to the tree house a few minutes later, Zack was sitting there silently in the dark. I knew something was up because he'd stopped doing his home-work. I grabbed my flashlight and leveled the beam in his face. He didn't even blink.

"Zack, are you all right?"

He nodded.

"Are you sure? You look . . . different."

He nodded again, very slowly, like he was working out some complicated thought in his head. Then he said in a croaky voice, "I think . . . something amazing just happened to me. Luke, I've changed."

Now, this didn't come as a great surprise. About six months before, Dad had taken me aside for what he called a man-to-man chat. We sat in his shed—I think that's because it's the most manly room we have—and Dad explained that from now on I might notice some changes in my big brother.

"Zack's embarking on a great journey," said Dad.

"Great! When's he leaving? Can I have his room?"

"Not that kind of journey," said Dad with a weary sigh. "He's going through something called puberty," he went on. "His voice will be different, for instance."

"Ooh, will he sound like a Dalek?"

"No, not like a Dalek."

"Bummer."

"He will become hairier."

"Ooh, like a werewolf?!"

"No, not like a werewolf."

This puberty deal didn't seem up to much. There was other stuff, to do with privacy and girls, but to be honest, after the letdown about the Dalek and the werewolf I stopped taking it in.

So, when Zack told me in the tree house that something had changed, I knew exactly what to say. I pursed my lips and gave a serious nod like I'd seen the doctor do when he told me I had strep throat. "I'm afraid that you have caught puberty."

He ignored me and stared at his hands, turning them over and over. "I think I have superpowers."

ZORBON

At first, I was sure Zack had gone completely bonkers—too much homework will do terrible things to a boy's mind. But then I grew suspicious. He knew how much I liked comic books and was constantly making fun of me for what he called my childish obsession. I smelled an ambush.

"Superpowers?" I folded my arms and sneered. "What, so now you can fly and shoot lightning from your fingertips?"

A curious expression spread across his face. "I wonder," he mused, sticking out one hand and flaring his fingers at me like some cheesy magician. Lightning did not shoot from his fingertips. But I was too stunned to notice, since something equally remarkable was happening.

My flashlight flew out of my grip, spun through the air, and landed in Zack's outstretched palm with a slap. His fingers closed around it, and he grinned.

Im-poss-ible!

But Zack had done it. He had made the flashlight move just by thinking about it and doing a lame hand gesture. Somehow it was true. My brother had an actual superpower!

What he'd done was called telekinesis, to give it its official title. Lots of superheroes have this ability in comics, but this was the first time I'd seen it in real life. I hated to admit it, but it was cool. Supercool. Not that I was going to tell Zack that.

"No lightning bolts, then," I said, pretending to be disappointed.

"What?!" He looked at me like I was stupid. "Did you *see* that? Did you see what I did?"

I couldn't keep up the pretense—I was impressed. But my awe quickly gave way to something else. I was as green as the Hulk; more jealous even than last Christmas when my parents gave Zack an iPhone, and I got shoes.

"It's not fair! How come you get superpowers? You don't even read comics." I ranted for a few more minutes—when I get going I have been known to turn purple—and then, finally exhausted, I flopped down on the floor and felt my face crumple into a sulk. Although I was seething with envy I had to know. "How did it happen?"

Zack stared past me, his eyes fixed on some hazy spot

on the wall, and began to describe the incredible—and incredibly recent—events.

"Just after you left I heard this distant rumbling noise, and so I looked out of the tree house. There were lights in the sky, and I thought it might be a meteor shower. And then I realized it was heading this way—fast. The sky was filled with hundreds of glowing white vertical lines. But just as they were about to hit, they came to a sudden stop. Then I saw that it was no meteor shower . . ."

He paused and drew a long breath before saying in a whisper, "It was a transdimensional spacecraft."

I gasped. Up until then the most exciting story Zack had ever told me involved a bad haircut and a Chihuahua. And I'm not convinced he was telling the truth about the Chihuahua.

"It was a large blue oval hanging in thin air, right outside there." He extended a trembling finger and pointed. "As I watched, a door in the side of the craft slid open with a sound like *bloop-whoosh*, and a luminous figure emerged on a beam of light. He wore a shiny purple suit, a cape with a high gold collar, and gold boots. On his chest were three gold stars that pulsed like heartbeats. He had a dome-shaped head, which was completely bald, and a wispy beard that he stroked when he spoke. He gave me a three-fingered salute and introduced himself as Zorbon the Decider, an interdimensional traveler and representative of the High Council of Frodax Wonthreen Rrr'n'fargh. Everything he said sounded like he was talking in all capitals. Zorbon explained that he came from another universe that exists in parallel to ours. It's almost exactly the same as our universe, he said, except there the colors green and red are reversed, and sponge cake tastes different." Zack looked thoughtful. "Not entirely different, just a little different."

I could tell by his daydreamy look that Zack found this boring fact particularly fascinating and there was a significant danger that he'd keep talking about sponge cake.

"Never mind about the stupid cake!" I said. "Get to the superpowers!"

Zack shook himself out of his trance. "Oh, yeah. Well, Zorbon said that I'd been chosen by the High Council for a mission of utmost importance to both our universes. A mission so vital that were I to fail, the consequences would be cataclysmic for *trillions* of beings."

"Two universes? You have to save *two* universes?" Typical. My brother was such an overachiever. "But why you?" I wailed.

Zack stared thoughtfully out of the door. "Apparently this tree house is the junction between the two universes."

This was incredible. Mind-blowing. Our tree house, a

portal between two worlds. On the other hand . . . "So?"

Zack shrugged. "I guess I was the first person Zorbon met when he came through."

I was speechless. My mouth moved, but no words came out, just a sound like air escaping from a balloon. That's not how you choose a savior of mankind. There has to at least be a prophecy written in an ancient book. This was like giving the Sword of Ultimate Power to a goldfish.

"To ensure my success," Zack continued, "Zorbon said he was authorized to bestow upon me six gifts—powers, if you like—to aid me in my cause. Then he raised his palms, said something in this really weird alien language—"

What, as opposed to a really *normal* alien language? I thought it but didn't say anything.

"There was this flash of red light—or maybe that should be *green* light," Zack went on. "I felt a surge of energy through my whole body. Every atom of my being was on fire. When it finally stopped, Zorbon bowed and said, 'IT IS DONE.' I asked him what was done. What powers had he bestowed? What was my mission? He said, 'I MUST NOT SAY. FOR IF I DO I RISK ALTERING THAT WHICH IS TO BE. AND AS ANYONE WHO UNDERSTANDS THESE KINDS OF SITUATIONS WILL TELL YOU, THAT WOULD BE A VERY BAD THING.

ALL WILL BECOME CLEAR. IN TIME.' Then he gave me this enigmatic smile and left. But just before the door of his craft slid shut, he said there was one thing he could tell me. This really scary look came over him, and he said, 'NEMESIS IS COMING.' And then he was gone. *Bloop-whoosh!*"

I stood there with my mouth wide open. So much to make sense of. So many questions. However, one thought pushed its way to the front of the line. "But I was only gone five minutes!" The most important five minutes in the history of the world, and I'd missed it because I needed to pee.

"I bet if I'd been here, Zardoz the Decoder would have chosen me," I grumped.

"His name was Zorbon the Decider. And you weren't here." Zack shrugged. "Should have held it in, huh?"

It was so unfair! I was way beyond acting like a normal, sensible person. "Get him back. Tell Bourbon the Diskdriver he made a mistake and he has to come back and give me superpowers too."

"Zorbon the Decider," corrected Zack once more. "And he decided I was the one. Not you."

"I don't believe you. We can't know for sure unless you call him."

"Call him? Oh, yeah, because he left his phone number. Uh, what's the area code for the parallel universe again?"

I detected a note of sarcasm in the question. Zack was teasing me, which was a rash thing to do given that at that moment I was more furious than I'd ever been in my entire life.

"What are you doing now?" he asked.

I stalked around the tree house, tapping the walls every few feet. "Searching for the portal to the other universe." I pressed one ear to the back wall. "I think I can hear it."

"Luke."

"Shh!" I hissed. I could definitely make out a sound. "Yes. Something's coming through. Sounds like scratching. Could be interdimensional mice."

"Uh, Luke . . ."

I spun around. The scratching sound was coming from Zack. He clawed at his chest through his shirt. As usual, he was still wearing his school uniform because he said it put him in the right frame of mind for homework. (I know. And I have to live with him.) Something weird was going on underneath. I screwed up my face and pointed. "What's that?"

A soft glow pulsed beneath the material like a night-light. He popped the buttons, gripped each half of his shirt, and pulled it apart to reveal his bare chest beneath. I swear I could hear trumpets.

Despite what Dad had said, there was no hair, but

there was something else. Inked across his chest were three glowing stars.

"Zorbon had stars just like these," said Zack. "I wonder what they mean." He ran a finger over them.

"I'll tell you exactly what they mean. They mean you've got a tattoo." I shook my head. "Mom's going to kill you."

Zack ignored me. He straightened, drawing himself up to his full five feet and three inches, and a calm, thoughtful expression came over his face. "I know what the stars mean," he breathed. "I. Am. Starman!"

I raised a finger of objection.

"What?" he snapped.

"Uh, sorry, but there's already a Starman. You'll probably get sued."

Zack gave a huff of irritation. "Fine. Whatever." He drew himself up again. "I. Am. Star Boy!"

He swiveled his eyes toward me, just to make sure. I gave a little shake of my head.

He threw up his hands in frustration. "There's a Star Boy, too?"

"I've told you a million times, you should read more comics." I tapped my cheek thoughtfully. Naming a superhero was harder than it looked.

"How about Star Guy?" said Zack.

"Star *Guy*?"

He rolled the name around his mouth a few times, trying it on for size. He said it in his own voice and then in a deep voice, and then he paused. "Star Guy or Starguy?"

He was serious.

"You can't call yourself Star Guy!" I objected.

"Why not?"

"Because there isn't a single superhero in history called 'guy.' That's why not."

He shrugged. "So I'll be the first." He planted his hands on his hips. "I. Am. Star Guy!" Then he angled his head thoughtfully. "Or perhaps Starguy. I. Haven't. Decided. Yet."

And that's how it happened. My brother is super-powered, and I . . .

. . . I am powerless.

STAR GUY

The fate of two universes lay in my brother's hands. In my hands was a cauliflower.

It was the day after Zack became Star Guy—he'd rejected Starguy, figuring if at some point he needed an insignia to put on a shirt, "S" was already taken. We were in the kitchen helping with dinner.

"Zack, darling, peel the potatoes." Mom handed him a large bag.

I caught his eye and grinned. Even superheroes have to peel potatoes.

"Of course." He beamed. "It'd be my pleasure."

He gave me a sly look and shuffled off to a corner of the kitchen. He was up to something. I crept up behind him. His eyes were narrowed at the potatoes, one hand extended toward them. The potato skins were falling off in perfect, unbroken spirals. They were peeling themselves.

I was shocked. "You can't do that," I hissed.

"Why not?"

"First rule of being a superhero: you can't go around using your powers for vegetable preparation."

He screwed up his face. "I doubt that's the first rule. Or any rule."

"No, well, maybe not, but with great power comes great responsibility. Gordon the Dishwasher—"

"Zorbon the Decider." Zack sighed.

For some reason I had a mental block about the name. I think it was because I was massively miffed about what he'd done and couldn't bring myself to remember his stupid alien extradimensional name.

"Yes, Whatshisname the Whatever. He didn't give you telekinetic abilities so you could help in the kitchen."

Zack looked sheepish. "You're right."

"Of course I'm right. Trust me, you don't want to abuse your powers. It's a slippery slope from superhero to supervillain. Sure, it starts innocently enough, peeling potatoes with telekinesis, but the next thing you know you're holed up in a secret volcano base with an army of evil minions and plans for world domination."

Just then Mom called across the kitchen. "What are you two plotting, hmm?"

"Nothing," we said at the same time.

Of course we couldn't tell her what had happened to

Zack. The second rule of being a superhero is that you have to keep it a secret. If the villains find out your real identity, then they lure you into a trap by kidnapping your loved ones. It's pretty basic stuff, and easily avoidable if you take simple precautions.

Mom and Dad gave each other these really lame smiles, and then Dad said, "Boys, it's really nice to see you two getting along."

It was true. Not that it was nice, but that Zack and I hadn't been getting along for some time. We used to be best friends when we were younger, but these days we mostly communicated by yelling, slamming doors, and giving each other dead arms. In fact, we'd probably talked more since last night than we had in the past three months. I caught him looking at me with this sad expression, like he missed the old days.

"What are you looking at, turnip head?" I said.

Oh, come on. I had to do something. The situation was in real danger of turning mushy.

Thankfully, Zack responded by punching me in the arm. It didn't break or fall off, which meant that superstrength wasn't one of his six powers. Interesting. I picked a point on his chest, drew back my fist, and threw a punch of my own. From this range I couldn't miss. And I didn't.

I bounced.

When my fist got within a few inches of his body, I felt it hit something springy and invisible.

"A force field! You've got a freaking force field!" I whispered in amazement.

Before I could say anything else, Dad pulled us apart, gave us a lecture on appropriate behavior, and sent us out of the kitchen to cool down.

Fifteen minutes later dinner was ready. All through the meal I watched Zack like a teacher in an exam room, waiting for him to push his cauliflower across his plate with his mind or flick a pea off his force field. Or . . . what else? Zebedee the Doolally had given him six powers that he needed for his mission. Telekinesis and a force field were two; what were the other four? And what about the mission? All we knew was that "NEMESIS IS COMING."

After dinner, when I was supposed to be doing my homework on the computer, I decided to poke around on the Internet and see what I could find out about Nemesis. There was a lot of information. I sifted through pages and pages of the stuff before reaching my conclusion.

In Greek mythology, Nemesis was, and I quote, "a remorseless spirit of divine retribution." I didn't understand all of it, but this Nemesis guy sounded pretty bad to me. Then it hit me like a thunderbolt: Nemesis had to be the name of a supervillain, and Zack had been given powers to defeat him.

I was about to navigate away from the page when I noticed something. I had read the entry too quickly. He wasn't a "he" at all. Nemesis was a girl! Well, that made perfect sense to me.

Star Guy's archenemy was a girl.

HI-MAD ORK

It was still light when Zack and I snuck out to the tree house to discuss my findings. I was carrying a Professor X tote bag that bulged mysteriously. Zack scampered up the rope ladder, and I huffed and puffed behind him. When I reached the top I sat in the doorway to catch my breath.

The sky was the color of streaky bacon. A breeze blew across the rooftops of the neighboring houses and rustled the leaves of the oak tree in our yard. We have a tiny yard, just a scrap of lawn, a border with some pink and blue flowers that come out in summer, a shed, and a huge oak tree. Dad says in the olden days our street was part of a giant forest full of black oaks. The tree in our yard is the only one left.

Dad built the tree house for us the previous summer. And when I say Dad built it, what I mean is that Grandpa built it, and Dad stood around in a tool belt with a lot of expensive gadgets, making unhelpful suggestions. He's keen on DIY, my dad, but the only thing he's ever successfully nailed to a wall is his thumb.

I joined Zack inside and told him everything I'd discovered about Nemesis. He listened carefully, nodding at my deductions like I was Sherlock Holmes. Ordinarily, my big brother would never listen to anything I have to say, but I'm an expert on superheroes (the ones in comics anyway), and he paid attention to every word. It was nice to be the smarter brother for a change.

"One more thing," I added. "I know how to activate your powers."

"You do?" He sounded impressed.

I nodded. "Yup, you just have to say your secret phrase."

Zack's eyes widened. "And you know my secret phrase?"

"I entered several factors into the computer—your name, known powers, shoe size—and this is what I've come up with. You ready?"

He nodded quickly. "Just tell me already!"

I cleared my throat. "Your secret activation phrase is . . ." I paused, like a reality show judge deciding who to put through to the next round. "*Hi-mad Ork.*"

Zack stood with his legs shoulder width apart and planted his hands on his hips before uttering the words.

"Hi-mad Ork!" He held his breath and waited. When after a few seconds nothing happened, he shook his head disappointedly. "I don't feel any different. Are you sure it's the right phrase?"

I stroked my chin. "Hmm. Maybe you're not saying it with enough feeling. Try it again, but this time really mean it and say it over and over."

"OK. More feeling. Over and over. Got it." Zack assumed the same pose. "Hi-mad Ork . . . Hi-mad Ork . . ." As he repeated the phrase it became clear what he was actually saying. "I'm a dork . . . I'm a dork . . . I'm a—"

I couldn't hold a snigger in any longer.

Zack's mouth froze in the shape of an "O" as he realized I'd tricked him. He glowered at me and said, "If you're going to act like a child, then I'm leaving." He marched out and put a foot on the top rung of the rope ladder.

"No, don't go. I promise I won't do anything childish again. From now on it's serious scientific investigation."

"You promise?"

I put a hand on my heart. "Promise."

He moved back inside, and I waved at him to stop. "Now stand there," I said, reaching into my tote bag. "And don't move."

"Why d'you want me to stand— Hey!"

He ducked as a tomato whistled over his head, landing with a *splat* against the wall behind him.

"What d'you think you're doing?"

I detected a note of irritation in his voice but ignored it, dug once more into my bag, and this time drew out a clipboard.

And a rock.

Zack had a force field, and we had to know how powerful it was. Clearly the easiest way to find out was to throw things at him. The bag concealed my battery of test objects.

"How can I put this?" I weighed the rock in my hand, tossed it up and down in my palm a few times, and then threw it hard at him.

He ducked once more, and the rock thudded against the wall. I let out a huff of frustration. "How am I supposed to test your force field if you keep ducking?" I made a note on the clipboard: Tomato and rock—inconclusive.

Zack started to get the picture. "I see. OK, that makes sense. I guess." He nodded toward my bag. "What else have you got in there?"

I'd been saving the best for last. With a grin I reached in with both hands and lifted out a sledgehammer. It was Dad's. I call it Thor's hammer.

"No way," Zack protested, flapping his hands in a frankly unheroic manner. "You're not throwing that thing at me."

"Of course I'm not going to throw it, idiot."

Zack relaxed.

"It's much too heavy to throw." I smiled thinly. "So I'm going to swing it at you."

Before he could object I drew the hammer back behind me and then, with all my strength, swung it in a long arc at my brother. Zack's protective field deflected the fat steel head like someone flicking a piece of fluff off their sleeve. The hammer rebounded, jarring my hands with a shuddering vibration so violent that I lost my grip. It flew narrowly over my head, straight out of the open door, and tumbled from sight. From somewhere in the undergrowth below, there was a thud followed by a strangled "meow."

"Did you hear that?" said Zack.

"Yes." I winced. "I think it was Mrs. Wilson's cat."

"No, not that," said Zack, closing his eyes tightly. "That."

I strained to listen, but all I could hear was the wind in the oak tree. "I don't hear anything," I began and then realized what that must mean. "You have super hearing."

Zack frowned. "Sort of. Although, it's more like a radar in my head. When I close my eyes I see this glowing green circle that sweeps around and around, and wherever there's a person or an object of interest they light up, and then I can see and hear them. It's not high-definition. All I can make out is a blurry outline." He blanched. "Uh-oh."

"What?"

"Someone's in distress."

I cringed. "Maybe Mrs. Wilson just found her cat."

A peculiar expression came over Zack, and his cheeks flushed as red as the tomato sliding gently down the wall. "It's not Mrs. Wilson," he said, his voice going up and down like a roller coaster.

"Then who is it?" I asked, but Zack didn't hang around to reply.

In a flash he was out the door, taking the rope ladder three rungs at a time. I scrabbled after him as fast as my flat feet would allow. He bounded down the path that ran along the side of our house, out toward Moore Street. I expected to find him fighting off a giant robot with laser beam eyes or a slimy alien horde, but when I got there a minute later Zack was nowhere to be seen. And instead of robots or aliens, there was something much more fearsome.

5

LARA AND CARA

It was a girl. And not just any girl. Her name was Cara Lee. Her family had moved in last year, two doors down from us, and she was in Zack's grade in school. She sat in front of him in math class. I knew that because I'd seen the drawings he'd made of her in the margins of his *Fun with Equations!* textbook. The drawings were all of the back of her head.

In person—from the front—she had big, brown eyes and long, dark hair, and she was tall—about three inches taller than Zack. A single stud earring shone from the top of her left ear. Earrings weren't allowed at our school, but Cara didn't even care. That made her a rebel. Though not like a Star Wars Rebel, which would have been even cooler.

Right then she was kneeling at the edge of the pavement, talking to a drain.

"Oh, please," she pleaded. "Don't be lost."

Perhaps she wasn't talking to the drain. Perhaps there was someone down there, trapped beneath the cover. She did have a younger sister called Lara who *could* have been hit by a shrink ray and then slipped through the grate.

On the first day of school I'd borrowed a uni-ball Gelstick Pen with a 0.4 mm tip from Lara and hadn't quite gotten around to returning it. Every time I bumped into her—on the street, in the hallway between classes—she'd ask me about it. She was annoying. Not enough for me to start making a list of her annoying points, but close.

Just then I saw Lara appear at the end of their driveway, which meant that she hadn't been zapped by a shrink ray and swept into the drain, unfortunately. Spotting her older sister, she marched over. Lara resembled Cara, except for her hair, which was cut short to reveal ears that made her look a bit like an elf or a Vulcan.

From where I stood I could make out what they were saying without the aid of super hearing.

"Mom sent me to get you," said Lara. "It's time to come in."

"I can't come in!" wailed Cara. "Oh, I'm in so much trouble."

"What's wrong?"

Cara turned unhappily to the drain. "I dropped my phone. It's down there. I can see it, but I can't reach it."

Before I knew what was happening, a hand grabbed my collar and hauled me behind Mrs. Wilson's garden wall. I let out a cry as my feet went out from under me.

"Shh!" Zack hissed. "You'll attract her attention."

I found myself down on the ground next to my brother. He had ducked out of sight and was peering intently at Cara over the wall.

I didn't understand what was going on. "Why are you hiding from her?"

"That's Cara Lee," he said breathlessly, as if that explained everything.

And then it hit me—the reason for Zack's odd behavior. He thought she was Nemesis! I peered over the wall to observe her. Could she be a supervillain?

"She has the eyes," I decided.

"I know," cooed Zack. "So . . . sparkly."

I was thinking more "evil," but whatever. So, was our neighbor Zack's archenemy? There was only one way to find out.

"Come on," I said, rising to my feet and motioning at him to follow.

"Where are you going? Get down before she sees you!"

"It's OK. I know exactly what you're thinking about Cara."

"You do?"

"Of course. And I have a plan. But we have to get close to her."

"Close? I can't get *close* to her. What if she . . . y'know?"

I understood completely. He was concerned that Cara might pull out a death ray or frazzle him with her fire breath.

"I know," I said. "But we have to take that risk."

"OK, but I can't just walk over there and start talking to her."

He was right. It would look too suspicious. We needed a reason to start a conversation. "She's lost her phone down that drain. You could use your telekinetic power to lift it out."

"You're right," he said, eyes bright, adding in a quivering voice, "and maybe she'll be so grateful that she'll"— he gulped and then squeaked—"kiss me."

Yes, I thought, a kiss of *death*. But I kept that to myself. I didn't want Zack any more nervous than he already seemed—which was jumpier than a kangaroo in a haunted trampoline factory.

"This will be an excellent field test of your superpowers," I said.

"Right. Powers. Test. Field."

"Just remember who you are."

"Zack Parker?"

Oh, dear. I took him by his shoulders and shook vigorously. "You're Star Guy."

"Yes. Star Guy. Me. Am."

We climbed over the wall, and I watched with a sinking feeling as Zack made his way awkwardly toward Cara. I sighed and ran to catch up. Without the benefit of my expertise, he was going to mess this up. However, I wanted to make one thing perfectly clear. "I'm not your sidekick, OK?" I said when I drew level with him.

Zack nodded. "OK."

Cara was bent over the metal grate, groaning and gasping as she tried to pull it off, so she didn't see Zack when he walked up and squealed, "Hi, Cara."

"Hi, Lara," I said.

She narrowed her eyes. "Where's my uni-ball Gelstick Pen with the 0.4 mm tip?"

As she said it I realized that if Cara was Nemesis, then Lara might be her accomplice and henchperson. I had to tread carefully. Before I could say anything Cara looked up and saw Zack.

"Oh. Hi," she said. "It's Jack, isn't it?"

"Yes," said Zack, grinning like a ventriloquist's dummy. I nudged him hard in the ribs. "Um, I mean no," he said. "It's Star—"

I nudged him again, harder. He was about to give away his secret identity—quite possibly to his archenemy!

"Zack. It's Zack," he said at last.

She studied him closely. If she was using an evil mind-reading power on him I couldn't detect it. "Don't you sit behind me in math?"

Zack's eyes bulged. "Yes. Yes, I do. And sometimes I stand behind you in the lunch line as well."

Cara exchanged a look with her sister. I'm no expert on girls, but I don't think it was a good look.

"Can I rescue you?" Zack blurted.

"What are you doing?" I whispered. "Are you *trying* to give away your superhero identity?"

Cara got to her feet. She towered over me and looked down on Zack. Her earring caught the last of the daylight and glittered like a deep space supernova. "You want to rescue me?"

He tried to smooth over his poor choice of words. "When I say rescue, I don't mean 'rescue.' That would be weird and possibly a bit unsettling. What I meant to say was 'help.' So, Cara who sits in front of me in math, can I help you?"

She shrugged. "I doubt it. I dropped my phone down there, so I don't think you can help, unless under that school shirt of yours you have really, really long arms."

Zack peered down his sleeves as if to check and then

said, "You know what, I think I do." He ushered her out of the way and knelt by the drain cover.

Now was my chance. My Nemesis test was a simple one. In comics some supervillains hide behind masks and rant about taking over the world, while others speak softly and wear boring business suits. But they all have one thing in common: their laugh.

Bwa-ha-ha-ha!

It stood to reason that if Cara Lee were an insane intergalactic transdimensional villain, then she would have a laugh just like that. So, all I had to do was make her laugh. This called for my best joke ever. I turned to the two girls. "What do you get," I began, "if you cross an elephant with a rhino?"

I could tell from their puzzled expressions that they were thinking about the answer, but then, disaster! Before I could hit them with the devastatingly funny punch line, there was a gurgle and a *whoosh* from behind me.

"Here you go. One *rescued* smartphone." Zack stood up, holding the phone triumphantly. He presented it to an amazed Cara.

She didn't even seem to mind that it was coated in something brown and bad-smelling.

"Thank you! Oh, thank you, Zack," she said, and then she laughed with relief.

It was less *bwa-ha-ha* and more *tinkle-tinkle*. No

self-respecting supervillain would laugh like that. So Cara wasn't Nemesis. "You're my hero!" She beamed.

A grin split my brother's face and kept on going, right around his ears and back again.

Cara cradled the precious phone. "But how on earth did you manage to reach it?"

He waggled his fingers and then said smoothly, "I'd tell you, but then I'd have to kiss you." He flushed. "*Kill* you. I meant I'd have to kill you. Not the other thing. Definitely kill you. Kill, kill, kill. Yup. That's the one."

Cara and Lara exchanged another of those suspicious sidelong looks. And at that moment I realized that Zack hadn't suspected Cara of being Nemesis at all. It was much worse than that—he *liked* her.

"C'mon, Lara," said Cara. "Mom'll be wondering where we are."

Zack watched Cara leave. I reckoned either he was studying the back of her head so he could make another drawing, or he was hoping that she'd turn around and smile at him again.

But she didn't.

"Well, not a total waste of time." I shrugged. "At least now we know you don't have heat vision."

He didn't take his eyes off her. "And how do we know that?"

"The way you're looking at Cara, if you had heat vision, you'd have melted her."

Zack looked crushed, and even though he was my brother I felt sorry for him. It was an old story, one I'd read a hundred times. Whether you're from planet Krypton or you use your billionaire fortune to fight crime in Gotham City, being a superhero messes up your love life.

CAPELESS

It was Monday night the following week, and Zack and I were talking in my bedroom. I don't normally let him—or anyone—into my room. Pinned to the door are various "Keep Out" signs, making clear the bloodcurdling fate that awaits trespassers. However, this was a special occasion.

"I'm not wearing that thing." Zack sniffed at the swishy rectangle of material I held out.

"But it's a cape." I was annoyed. I'd spent the whole weekend working on it, instead of doing my homework. "Every superhero needs a cape." I knew that wasn't strictly true, but my brother was the world's first *real* superhero. People would be upset if he didn't have a cape.

He folded his arms. "It's not a cape; it's one of the curtains from the downstairs bathroom."

I was hoping he hadn't noticed. "Yes, OK, maybe it does look a bit curtain-y." I held it up and smoothed the material, showing him the pattern. "But see, it's got stars. How perfect is that for Star Guy? It's like it was meant to be. As if eons ago the Guild of Cosmic Cape Makers knew that one day it would come to pass that a star-themed superhero would need the appropriate cape, and so they disguised it as an ordinary curtain and hid it in plain sight in the downstairs bathroom of a boring suburban house, waiting for the day . . ."

Zack gawped. "You're bonkers. You do know that, right?"

"Please wear it. Do you know how long I spent sewing in the Velcro fastener?"

He threw open a window, leaned on the sill, and looked back at me over his shoulder. "If you think I'm going out there in a costume made from a curtain, you're even crazier than I thought. Next thing you'll have me in a pair of Mom's tights."

My hand went to my pocket, and I made a mental note: Don't bring out the tights.

"But you have to wear some sort of costume," I said. "People expect it."

"Do they? Just because superheroes in comics wear stupid outfits doesn't mean I have to. That's your problem— you think everything's a comic. But this is real life, Luke. Time you got your head out of the fantasy world and look around you. You need to grow up."

I crossed to the open window in silence and gazed out at Moore Street bathed in the orange glow of the streetlamps. I looked up at my brother. "How about a mask?"

Zack groaned and threw up his hands. He began to pace back and forth, grumbling about curtain fabric and ridiculous superhero rules. My room isn't very big, and most of it is taken up by my inflatable solar system, which hangs from the ceiling. Casually, he stuck out a hand and used his telekinetic power to shove it aside, then stopped and clicked his fingers. "OK, I know what I'm going to wear. Wait here."

He slouched out of the room and returned five minutes later sporting a black hooded sweatshirt over a pair of black jeans and a pair of grubby old gray sneakers.

"So, what d'you think?" he asked, flipping the hood up so that it covered his face.

"That people'll think you're going to mug them, not save them." I didn't try to hide my disappointment. "It's not fair," I grouched. "If I was Star Guy, I'd do it properly. I'd wear the cape."

Zack wasn't listening. He adjusted his hood, pulling the cords sharply to cinch it together like a Venus flytrap closing around its lunch.

"At least take this," I said, handing him a metal pin decorated with a cluster of gold stars like the ones on his chest, arranged to form the letters "S" and "G" for Star Guy. The stars were from an old Christmas decoration, and I'd glued them to one of Mom's brooches. She had lots—she wouldn't miss one.

Zack poked his head out from his hood and examined it closely.

"It's a brooch," he said, unimpressed.

"No," I corrected him. "It's a 'sigil.' That's what superheroes call a logo."

I could see that he was considering accepting it. "You need something to identify yourself as Star Guy. Come on, Zack, it's cool."

"It *is* cool," he conceded, pinning it to his chest. He turned to admire his reflection in a small mirror that was part of my alien invasion–busting, laser-destructor diorama. I was building a scale-model high-orbit energy weapon. Just for fun. It was nonfunctioning, unfortunately. Zack licked a finger and smoothed his eyebrows.

"So, what now?" he said.

"What do you mean?"

"I've got the powers, I've got the costume. You're the expert—what happens now?"

He really was clueless. There was only one possible path for a newbie superhero to take.

"Now," I said, with a little smile, "you fight crime."

He frowned. "How? I mean, I know there's crime out

there." He waved vaguely out of the window. "But where *exactly*?"

For flip's sake, did I have to draw him a diagram? "Use the radar thingy in your head."

"Oh, yeah . . ." Zack shut his eyes and then said, "Wow!"

"What happened?"

"It just lit up like a Christmas tree. Hang on. Some of the incidents are brighter than others. I'm zooming in on the brightest."

"What can you see?"

"It's the bakery on Bank Street."

Stolen buns. OK, it wasn't much, but it was a start.

"No, wait," said Zack. "It's the *bank* on *Baker* Street."

I rubbed my hands together excitedly. "A bank heist! Now we're talking." I marched to the door and pulled my coat down off the hook.

"Come on," I said. "What are we waiting for?"

Zack stood in the center of my room, shifting from foot to foot. "It's ten miles away. How do I get there?"

Some superheroes could fly. Some could run incredibly fast. Others were able to teleport from place to place in the blink of an eye.

"We could take the bus?" I suggested.

"The bus takes forever," he said, kicking his heels. "The robbers will have finished before I even get there."

"We could bike it?"

"Nah, my bike's got a slow puncture." I could hear the enthusiasm leak out of him like air from his deflating tire.

"And anyway," he added, "Mom's never going to let either of us out on a school night."

It was true. I sat down heavily on my bed and rested my head in my hands. The villains of the world were safe from the wrath of Star Guy, unless they committed their crimes between the hours of 3:45 p.m. and 5:30 p.m. on weekdays. Quite near to our house.

But on weekends and holidays they were in trouble. Oh, yeah. Big trouble!

Unless, that is, they were up early.

Zack had Speech & Drama first thing Saturday mornings, and on Sundays Dad insisted that we help him in the shed on a DIY project. Currently, we were helping him make a plate rack for the kitchen.

"If we tell Mom and Dad about my superpowers," Zack said thoughtfully, "then maybe they'd give me a ride?"

"You want Mom and Dad to drop you off at the scene of the crime?"

"Yeah."

"That's a terrible idea," I said. "I mean, think about it. Do they wait in the car while you stop the bank robbers?

Does Mom go off and do some shopping? What if Dad can't find a parking spot? He'd have to drive around and around until you're finished, and he hates that."

Just then, Mom called up from downstairs, bringing our chat to an end. Barely five minutes ago I was about to embark on a thrilling adventure with my superhero brother. Now, instead of having the time of my life foiling a bank heist, it was bath time.

THE LEGEND BEGINS

It was 2:47 p.m. the following Saturday when Zack finally did something properly heroic. I know it was exactly 2:47 because we'd just been to Crystal Comics and were waiting at the bus stop right outside it on Main Street. For the first time ever I'd persuaded Zack to come with me to the comic store, telling him if he wanted to understand how to be a superhero, then who better to teach him than Spider-Man and Batman? Afterward, clutching a bundle of new comics, we waited for the 55 bus. It was due at 2:47. And it was on time.

"That's unusual," I remarked.

"It's not that unusual," said Zack, who took more buses than me. "The 55 is actually quite punctual."

"I don't mean that," I said, pointing. "Look."

The bus hurtled down the road, swerving wildly from side to side, its horn blaring like a frightened animal. It bounced off the curb, sending people on the pavement fleeing in terror, then tore past a line of cars waiting at the light, snapping their side mirrors like a giant pulling wings off flies. As it plunged toward us I saw the driver wrestling with the wheel, his face white with fear.

In a flash I guessed what had happened. "The brakes have failed!"

The door to the comic book store flew open, and a gaggle of boys poured out to see what all the commotion was about.

The bus clipped a parked car and went up on two side wheels. A hubcap shot off like a Sidewinder missile, flying over the head of a police officer and crashing through the window of the hardware store. The bus was half on its side, its metal bodywork screeching against the road, leaving a trail of sparks behind it like a lit fuse to a bomb.

"Zack," I whispered, "you have to do something."

He flipped up his hood and strode purposefully out into the middle of the road, directly into the path of the oncoming bus.

A few of the boys from the comic book store started to point.

"Look at that idiot!"

"What's he doing?"

"He's going to get himself killed!"

The last speaker, a red-haired boy with freckles,

whipped out his cell phone, tapped the video camera icon, and began to record.

Zack planted his feet and stretched out both arms. He was going to use his telekinetic power to stop the runaway vehicle. I'd seen him use it to move a flashlight and peel a potato, but they were nothing compared to a city bus. I almost couldn't look. He lowered his head, concentrating fiercely, summoning his superpower.

The bus kept on coming. The noise of tearing metal-work was dreadful. And then, just as it seemed about to flatten Zack, something incredible happened.

The nose of the bus rose up, quickly followed by the rest. Zack stood there, arms extended like a weight lifter, the enormous vehicle hovering above his head.

Main Street on a Saturday afternoon was a noisy place, but at that moment it fell utterly silent, save for the creaking of the suspended bus and the squeak of its spinning wheels.

The sidewalk was filled with gawking pedestrians. Drivers stopped their cars to stare in slack-jawed amazement.

Zack lowered the bus gently to the ground. The excitement was too much for the old vehicle. There was a groaning of joints, and its suspension sagged. The hydraulic doors opened with a sigh like a dying breath, and the passengers emerged on unsteady legs, dazed but otherwise perfectly unharmed.

The comic store boys were the first to find their tongues. Like me, they'd been waiting their whole lives for something like this to happen.

They started to cheer madly.

The rest of the street joined in, applauding and whooping.

I stood at the edge of the crowd of cheering boys, not that any of them paid me the slightest attention. They were almost hysterical with excitement.

"Did you see that?"

"That was incredible!"

"Who is he?"

I covered my mouth and coughed, "Star Guy."

"I think he's called Star Guy," said one.

"Star Guy? Cool," said one more.

"Shame he doesn't have a cape," said another. I gritted my teeth.

"D'you think he'd sign my comic?" wondered the red-haired boy with freckles.

As soon as he suggested the idea, the whole bunch seemed to decide it was a very good one, and they all ran toward my brother waving their latest issues of Justice League and X-Men. I tagged along. Not that I hoped to get his autograph; I just wanted to make sure Zack didn't mess up his first contact with the public. As I drew closer I recognized a face among the last passengers to leave the broken bus. It was Cara Lee. Still stunned from her ordeal, as she stepped off she missed her footing and slipped. With a yell, she tumbled right into Star Guy's arms.

"I've got you, miss."

I don't think Zack recognized her at first, but as he set her back on her feet they were face to face—or face to hoodie—and he saw with a start who it was he'd rescued.

"Thank you," she breathed.

He ducked his head, and she shot a curious glance at her hooded savior. For a moment I was sure that she'd recognized him as her slightly weird neighbor.

"Have we met before?" she asked.

"Uh, I . . . we . . . um . . ."

Thankfully, at that moment Zack was swamped with people clamoring for his attention and Cara was carried away in the crush.

"Star Guy!" cried one of the comic store boys, brandishing a copy of The Amazing Spider-Man. "You're . . . amazing!" he added, rather unimaginatively.

"Wow! The way you stopped that bus," said another, mimicking Star Guy's stance and hand action, adding his own sound effects. "*GRRRRAUNCH!* You used gravity manipulation, right?"

"No," said another scornfully, "bet it was magnetism."

"Baloney," said the next boy. "It was wind."

The others looked at him questioningly. "Wind?"

He shrugged, a little embarrassed. "Wind . . . control. Obviously."

"Why are you wearing a brooch?" asked the red-haired boy.

"It's not a brooch," said Star Guy tightly. "It's a 'sigil.'"

"Ooooh," said all of the comic store boys.

The policeman whose hair had been parted by the flying hubcap politely but firmly pushed his way through the excited crowd. He wanted a statement from the hero of the hour. A burly fellow with a red face, he took out a pencil and notebook.

"Name, please."

"Za—" began my brother, then saw me making a cutthroat motion. "Star Guy," he half screeched, half growled.

In the tree house earlier that week we'd discussed how he should talk when he found himself in public as Star Guy. I told him it was important to disguise his voice so that no one could identify him as Zack Parker, and so he tried out a few different voices before settling on a deep, rumbly one. The only problem was puberty. Dad had been right about that—Zack's voice did change, often in the middle of sentences. It croaked up and down like a frog tied to a firework.

The cop made a face. "Say that again."

I knew Zack was blushing under his hoodie. He cleared his throat and tried again. "Star Guy."

The cop scratched a note in his book. "First name, Star. Last name, Guy."

Zack started to correct him. "No, I didn't mean—never mind."

"Would you mind removing your hood, Mr. Guy?"

"No," said Zack quickly. "I can't do that."

"Why not?" asked the policeman.

"Uh . . . um . . ." he stuttered.

Uh-oh, I thought. We hadn't talked about what to do if this happened. Zack was going to blow it—I could tell. In two seconds the world would know his real identity. I couldn't look.

"I'm horribly disfigured," he said at last. "I fell into a vat of chemicals, and my face is, y'know, too ugly to be seen in public. Yeah, that's what happened."

Not bad. Not bad at all. I'd never have thought of that so quickly. I did have one criticism, which was that, traditionally, falling into a vat of chemicals created a supervillain, not a hero, but I'd let that pass.

"Horribly disfigured, you say?" repeated the policeman,

squinting and leaning in to steal a glimpse behind Zack's hood.

Zack drew sharply on the cords that closed his hood. It came down like a steel shutter. "Yes," he said flatly. "Hideous."

The policeman drew back and coughed, a little embarrassed. He made a show of starting a fresh page in his notebook. "So, Mr. Guy, can you explain how you, umm . . ." He waggled his pencil with the air of a man who knows he's about to ask something very, very silly, but can't help himself because rules are rules. "How you . . . made the bus rise into the air?"

"Telekinesis," said Zack.

Around him, most of the crowd murmured in amazement. However, the comic book boys nodded knowingly.

"Ri-i-ight," said the policeman with a doubtful expression, his pencil poised over his notebook. "And how are you spelling that?"

There was no time for Zack to answer because just then a voice rang out from the crowd.

"Where is he? Where is the wonderful young man who saved my life?"

The voice belonged to a tiny white-haired old lady. She was wearing a purple-and-yellow-spotted dress that looked like an outbreak of some nasty disease and using a walker like a battering ram to muscle her way to the front of the crowd, leaving a trail of stepped-on toes and knocked ankles.

She stood before Zack. "I want to give you something," she said, rummaging in a handbag the size of a small moon.

"That's really not necessary, madam," he said, holding up a hand. "I don't accept cash or gift tokens. I do this for the good of all mankind."

We'd rehearsed that. The bit about "mankind" was mine.

But the old lady wasn't reaching for her wallet. Instead, she fished out a lipstick, which she popped open and smeared across her wrinkly lips. She puckered them for a kiss. "I'm ninety-three, you know."

The crowd watched expectantly. That's the problem with old people—they get away with anything because they're nearly dead.

I knew that Zack had fantasized about rescuing Cara Lee and being rewarded with a kiss. The reality was seventy-nine years older and a whole lot crinklier. He dipped his head so that the old lady was enveloped by his hood. There was an awful slurping from within.

As one, the comic book boys winced and made a sound like sour milk circling down the drain. But everyone else cheered. Clearly, this is what the public wanted from their superheroes: to rescue Saturday shoppers from runaway buses and kiss old ladies. Cell phone cameras snapped the moment. I think I even saw someone throw a hat in the air. It was either a hat or a hamster.

And that's how it happened. Thanks to poor maintenance of the 55 bus, and Mrs. Doris Stevens, ninety-three—of Station Road, across from Loon Fung Chinese Takeout—the legend of Star Guy was born!

8

SECRET IDENTITY

The boy with red hair and freckles, who'd recorded Star Guy's heroic act on his cell phone, uploaded the video right away. Within minutes the footage, entitled "Star Guy versus the 55," had attracted thirty hits. An hour later the number of views reached three thousand. By the end of the day, over a quarter of a million people had watched my big brother stop a runaway bus using telekinesis. By the end of the week, Star Guy was bigger than the cutest cat on the Internet, and second only to a Hawaiian dance craze that was sweeping the globe, or at least the areas of it with nothing better to do than gather in large numbers and perform something called the "Hula Robot."

In the comments sections of hundreds of blogs and websites, you could read the same furious argument. There were people who believed that the video was real—that they were watching a real superhero with real powers. And then there were other people convinced that the video was part of a viral advertising campaign for some new Hollywood blockbuster.

I wasn't annoyed that these people didn't believe in Star Guy. I felt sad for them. They'd rather look for reasons to call him a fake than believe he was real.

"Dad, why do they say Star Guy doesn't exist?" I asked one morning over breakfast.

Zack gave me a hard stare. He didn't like it when I talked superhero stuff in front of Mom and Dad, in case anything slipped out. Dad spooned a mouthful of cornflakes without lifting his head from his newspaper. "They're called 'skeptics,'" he said between crunches.

"Skeptics?" I repeated. "They sound like a race of skinny aliens from a dying planet with dastardly plans for taking over Earth and turning everyone into human McNuggets."

Dad raised his spoon. "Or . . ." He waved it in a small circle. "Or, a skeptic might be someone who questions the facts, or what other people take for granted." He raised his eyebrows as if to say, "Might that be a better definition?"

"And it's fine to be a skeptic," he continued. "It's always good to question what people tell you."

I thought about that for a second. "Even what you tell me?"

"Ah," he said, his spoon dipping. "Ah . . ."

I saw him and Mom exchange looks and was glad I wasn't on the end of the one she gave him.

"Yes," said Mom. "You can question your *dad*. But never your mom. Under this roof it is the Undemocratic People's Republic of Mom, and I'm Supreme Leader. Don't you forget it."

Mom often said stuff like this. I think it was meant to be funny, but I didn't get it. Anyway, there were far more important things on my mind. "You believe Star Guy's real, don't you?" I looked to each of my parents in turn.

"I'd like to," said Dad. "The world could certainly do with a superhero."

"Well, whether he's a superhero or just a regular hero," said Mom, "Mrs. Lee from down the road is happy he was there. Her Cara was on that bus."

Zack perked up at the mention of her name. He'd had his head buried in an essay for history class, but now he peered curiously over the top of the notebook.

"Who knows what would've happened if that young man hadn't stopped it from crashing." Mom shook her head slowly at the terrible thought of what might have been. "Whoever he is, seems Cara can't stop talking about him."

There was a clatter and a crash next to me. Zack had knocked over his bowl. Milk and cereal oozed across the floor like blood and guts from a murder victim. He said sorry and went to fetch a cloth.

Mom pushed back her chair and started to collect the rest of the breakfast bowls. "OK, everybody. School for you two, down to the mines for us."

Mom and Dad didn't actually work in a mine. I'm not sure there even is a mine near us. But Mom thought it was funny to say so on a regular basis. I didn't get it. I think working in a mine would be highly interesting. You might find pirate treasure or disturb a sleeping, shape-changing horror with tentacles buried during the last ice age. But Mom and Dad worked together in an office for an insurance company.

Following that incredible Saturday afternoon, Zack knuckled down to mastering his powers. After school, we used the children's playground as a makeshift test facility. Zack used his radar power to check that no one was around to see us, then his telekinesis to make all the swings move at once. One by one, he added the rest of the equipment, whizzing the merry-go-round and tipping the seesaw, until the whole place looked as if it were being played on by ghosts. To test his force field I fired increasingly larger rocks down the slide at him. He deflected them all.

We knew that Zack had three more as-yet-unknown superpowers. The burning question was, could he fly? In my opinion a superhero who can't fly isn't in the Premier League. So that evening I decided to find out.

"Hey! Did you just try to push me out of the tree house?" said Zack, teetering on the edge of the doorway.

"No," I said. "Well, maybe a bit. I just want to know if you can fly. Aren't you curious?"

"Not enough to jump out of a tree fifteen feet off the ground."

I peered out investigatively. "You're right," I said. "It's not nearly high enough." I glanced across to the house. "We should go up to the roof."

"Are you trying to kill me?!" said Zack, backing away. "I bet that's it. You're still jealous that I got to be a superhero and you didn't."

He was right. I was still jealous and always would be. How could I not be? My brother was living *my* fantasy.

"You know what I think?" Zack went on. "I think you're Nemesis. *You're* my archenemy."

That would have been cool. I could hear the voice-over in my head. "Two brothers. Two paths. Destined to collide." But Zack was forgetting an important point.

"Nemesis is a girl," I reminded him.

Despite my insistence that it was for his own good, Zack refused to jump off the roof, which meant we were unable to confirm if he could fly. For now.

In the meantime he went on to perfect his radar power and fix the puncture on his bicycle, which meant he was able to respond to incidents up to ten miles away. In a single week he rescued a baby from a burning building, held a bridge together when it started to collapse during rush hour, and stopped a robbery in a jewelry store. He was on the front page of our local paper every day, and all over the national and international TV news. If you searched online, you could read articles and watch videos in dozens of different languages. Star Guy is *Estrella Muchacho* in Spanish, *Stjärna Pojke* in Swedish, and *Etoile Garçon* in French.

The one thing everyone wanted to know was his true identity. Who was the boy behind the hoodie? TV crews from all over the world had staked out Main Street, the mall, and the park in the hope of catching Star Guy in action. You couldn't buy a bag of M&M's in the corner store without Japanese Nightly News shoving a camera in your face and asking for a comment.

At school, Cara Lee had become even cooler than before. Ever since the other kids saw her on the video falling off the runaway bus into Star Guy's arms, she'd become a celebrity.

However, all of this talk about Star Guy posed a problem for me because I knew who he was. I knew that his favorite ice cream was Chunky Monkey. I knew that at the back of his drawer he kept a pair of Thomas the Tank Engine underpants that hadn't fit for years, but that he refused to throw out. I knew that in moments of high anxiety he still sucked his thumb.

And I couldn't tell a soul.

At first, it was oddly satisfying to know something that no one else did. And not just any old dull secret about who likes whom at school, or who keyed the principal's Kia—no, this was perhaps the greatest secret in the world. And it was mine and Zack's. Nobody else's. But with just the two of us to carry it around, it was a heavy secret—and as Star Guy became more famous, it was about to get much heavier.

9

SERGE

Keeping Zack's secret was particularly difficult at school, where my friends could talk about nothing else. My best friend, Serge, who's French and therefore starved of proper superhero role models, became obsessed with Star Guy. I'll admit it, I'm quite fanatical when it comes to superheroes, but Serge went completely nuts.

He drew Star Guy comic strips, wrote Star Guy fan fiction, and started up a Star Guy web forum. When we weren't at school he would wear a copy of Star Guy's costume, which was very confusing for me. From a distance I kept mistaking him for the real Star Guy, which pleased Serge no end, but which I knew could lead to me giving the game away by accident. All I had to do was shout out "Zack" one time by mistake and that would raise a whole lot of awkward questions.

Serge is shorter than me and has to use an inhaler for

his asthma. Although, I have to admit, when he does use it he inhales very stylishly.

"*Ffffft*," said Serge, taking a long suck of Ventolin.

It was Saturday morning, and we were on Main Street at the bus stop outside the comic book store. Once a week Serge insisted on coming to the spot where Star Guy had first blazed onto the scene. In history class we had learned about people who make long, tough journeys to special places as an act of worship. It's called a pilgrimage. That's what Serge was doing. Although the journey wasn't exactly long or tough, just half a dozen stops. And we always got ice cream afterward.

"It was at this very bus stop," said Serge in an awed tone, "where Star Guy used his *te-le-kin-etic* powers for the *premier* time in order to rescue the *bee-yoo-tiful* Cara Lee."

Somehow when people talked about that day they forgot about the old lady and the rest of the passengers. It was like they'd been written out of the story. Now the lasting image—printed on thousands of T-shirts and on posters stuck to thousands more bedroom walls—was of Star Guy catching Cara Lee when she tripped on the bottom step of the bus.

"Can you imagine what it must have been like to stand here and regard it as it happened?"

Obviously, I didn't have to imagine because I had been here. However, I'd discussed it with Zack, and we decided it would be safer not to tell people that I had witnessed Star Guy's debut. We didn't want a super-villain making a connection between my presence and Star Guy's true identity. There's a moment in the video taken that day when you glimpse me, but it's only my right hand—I'm clutching a wad of comics—and in none of the footage do you ever see my face.

There was a long, drawn-out squeak as Serge ran a moist hand down the plastic window of the bus shelter. "Per'aps Star Guy laid his hand against this very window."

Serge squinted up at the electronic passenger information board. "Per'aps Star Guy regarded this very electronic passenger information board."

Serge ducked inside the shelter and knelt to stroke the plastic seating. "Per'aps Star Guy sat his derriere on this very seat."

If only he knew how close he was to Star Guy. All right, Star Guy's little brother. But still, it would make his day. His year. His whole life! And really, what harm could it do if I told him? Just him, of course. And he couldn't tell anyone else. I could feel the words burning the tip of my tongue. I opened my mouth to speak, but instead of my secret out came a long sigh, and I said, "Are you done yet? Can we go?"

Serge stuck out his lower lip and shook his head. "Not yet. I have composed an oath."

"An oath?"

"*Oui*. Y'know, it is the thing a superhero says right before he does something super heroic." He cleared his throat, placed one hand on his chest and said:

> "Granted cosmic superpower
> In our darkest hour,
> Star Guy, star light,
> Protector of the world tonight."

It was terrible. Cheesier than a cheddar mine.

"So, what do you think?" asked Serge proudly.

I paused. "It's . . . interesting."

"It rhymes," he said, pleased with himself.

"Yes, I noticed that. Very rhyme-y. Just so I'm clear, you want Star Guy to say this? Out loud?"

"That is the idea."

"And how is he going to find out about it?"

"Repetition. I will say it. A lot. On my Star Guy discussion forums. Within my fan fiction. Star Guy is bound to notice, and then it will follow naturally."

It would never happen. There was no way Zack would say something as lame as Serge's terrible oath. "Great. That's great, Serge. Now can we go?"

He shook his head briskly. "Ah, *non*. I must now go in here."

He headed toward the comic book store. I hadn't been back since that day. If I'm honest, the thrill of reading stories about superheroes had faded since the arrival of Star Guy in my daily life. Reading comics used to be like going into another world. Now it was like going into our living room. It had become so bad that to escape from my everyday life I'd started to read books about ordinary children living hard, gritty lives in the projects, where the biggest drama is whether the hero gets on the football team or ends up being arrested for stealing cars.

Serge headed inside. I didn't know it, but as I followed him I was about to encounter the greatest threat that Star Guy had yet faced.

10

THE ADVENTURES OF STAR GUY

Crystal Comics was part of an empire. Not like the Galactic Empire or even the Roman Empire. There were twelve Crystal Comic shops dotted around the country, and I'm not sure what their policy was on taking over the world. So, a small empire. Although they were part of the same company, each shop was unique. Inside they were designed to look like ice fortresses or space stations or superhero hideouts.

The one on Main Street wasn't the biggest, but it was still spread over two floors, one of them underground. The entrance was like a futuristic check-in desk at a spaceport, where they pretended to scan you in case you posed a threat. It was pretty cool, although in my opinion they didn't have nearly enough security to stop you from getting in if you did actually turn out to be a dangerous Xenomorph with acid blood and a taste for human flesh.

Once inside, the space theme continued. The whole

place was designed to look like a moon base in the middle of an alien invasion. The ground floor was a series of connected pods, each filled with a dizzying array of blinking control panels and viewing windows displaying the inky black vacuum of outer space. Lights flickered, ceilings dripped with green alien snot. Shadowy shapes lurked behind access hatches whirring with fans. Computer screens flashed red with emergency distress signals. Wherever you went you could hear an eerily calm computer-generated woman's voice steadily counting down a self-destruct sequence, over and over again—which was highly atmospheric but must have been very annoying if you worked there. Oh, and there were comics. Lots of comics. Shelves full of the latest issues were cleverly built into the walls and floors.

On the lower floor, which you could only reach by shuttle craft (i.e., an elevator) the shiny, brightly lit moon base gave way to dripping caverns meant to look like some creepy dead alien civilization. There were lava pits and craters, and the floor was shrouded in a bright green mist pumped out of vents in the wall. There was a door marked AIRLOCK—AUTHORIZED PERSONNEL ONLY, which one of the salespeople once told me was the staff bathroom.

In a cavern at the back was an area called "Special Collections." In here were rare and expensive comics for rich collectors. On one wall, not for sale, was a framed copy of Action Comics No. 1—the most valuable comic in the world. But I think their copy was a copy, if you know what I mean. Above the frame was a laser gun, and there was a sign next to it saying that thieves would be vaporized. But it wasn't a real laser gun. If I had a genuine Action Comics No. 1, I'd have made sure the laser gun was fully functioning.

Everyone who worked at Crystal Comics wore the same uniform: a red jumpsuit crisscrossed with zippers and pockets, a black peaked cap with "CC" spelled out in gold, shiny black boots, and a gold belt with pouches containing useful things like price sticker guns and credit card scanners.

A red-uniformed security man studied Serge and me closely as we passed through the body scanner at Spaceport Check-in. The machine made a humming noise, and a bright blue light moved slowly from our heads to our feet. On top of the scanner a green light flashed, indicating that we were cleared to enter. It was all pretend, of course, but it gave every visit to the shop a sense of occasion, like you really were arriving aboard a far-flung moon base.

Across the room something caught Serge's attention. "Ah, this is what I came for!" he announced excitedly and bounced off to a corner of the shop where eager readers clustered around a long table manned by Crystal Comics employees.

It was the launch of a new title, always a big day in the comic fan's world, but particularly significant today. A poster above the table advertised "The Adventures of Star Guy."

Perhaps I was seeing things after the bright scanner light. I rubbed my eyes and looked again. It was true. While I'd been busy with the real Star Guy I hadn't noticed that someone else had created a comic book version to cash in on his fame. I pushed my way to the front of the line.

"You can't do this!" I fumed to the nearest Crystal Comic sales assistant, a wobbly ball of a man with a red jumpsuit that bulged like a wind sock full of watermelons. He just shrugged and kept on selling the debut issue. There were stacks of them, and they were going fast. I grabbed one and slammed it down on the table. "You're not allowed to sell stories about Star Guy."

"Says who?" said the wobbly sales assistant.

"Says me," I snapped.

He raised one eyebrow. "Oh, yeah? And who are you?"

"I'm . . . I'm . . ." Oh, I so wanted to tell him who I really was. That would shut him up double quick, but the words wouldn't come out.

"You're who?" he pressed. "No, wait. Don't tell me.

You're . . . Star Guy!" He sniggered, his chins quivering like acne-flavored jelly. The other sales assistants and most of the line joined in. They were all laughing at me.

"All right," he said, tired of the joke. "Either buy the comic or make way for someone who wants one."

Openmouthed with indignation, but powerless to do anything, I slunk off. Serge joined me a few moments later, clutching a copy of the comic. I couldn't believe he'd actually bought it, not after witnessing my outburst.

"How could you?" I asked.

He puffed out. "It is a comic. I am Star Guy's number one fan. How could I resist such a combination?"

Before I could object, there was a wail from the front of the shop. A red light flashed on top of the scanner. Something had set off the Alien Detection Warning System.

Standing in the unearthly glow was a figure in jeans, sneakers, and a white T-shirt with the words "Don't make me angry" spelled out in green letters.

It was Lara Lee.

"What's she doing here?" I asked Serge.

He shrugged. "Who can truly say? Women, they are mysterious. Even more mysterious than Mysterio."

Lara carried a battered leather satchel looped over one shoulder. The pretend security man signaled to her to hand it over. Reluctantly, she passed it to him for an inspection. As he rooted inside she shifted uneasily from foot to foot. He pulled out a World War II gas mask.

"What's this for?" He waved it in Lara's face.

"A gas attack," she said curtly.

"You expecting one of those?"

"Better safe than sorry."

He scowled and dug deeper into the satchel, this time producing a glass test tube stopped with a cork. Inside was a disgusting purple liquid. He peered at it with great suspicion.

"Is this a stink bomb?"

"What a preposterous suggestion," replied Lara.

"Then you won't mind if I have a quick sniff, will you?" His nose wrinkled in preparation. He reached for the cork.

"No!" Lara put her hand in the way. "You really don't want to do that."

"Didn't think so," said the security man smugly. "I think I'd better hang on to these items while you shop. *Madam*."

Lara started to object, but when she saw that it would do no good she slouched off, muttering darkly about human rights abuses. Then she caught sight of me and something strange happened.

"Hi, Luke," she said with a friendly smile.

You see? Weird. It was the first time in more than a

year that she'd greeted me with anything other than a question about the whereabouts of her uni-ball Gelstick Pen with a 0.4 mm tip.

Serge coughed politely to remind me he was standing there too.

"You know Serge, don't you?"

"Hi," said Lara.

Serge leaned casually against the nearest counter and took a pull on his inhaler. "Nice T-shirt," he said. "It brings out the color of your startling eyes."

Serge always knew what to say to girls. It was like a superpower. It seemed everyone had them, except me.

Lara looked hard at each of us in turn. I felt like I was being scanned all over again.

"I need your help," she said at last.

That was unexpected.

"You do?" I asked. "What for?"

She smiled slowly. "We're going to unmask Star Guy."

PLAN F

My *mouth went* dry. Lara Lee wanted me, of all people, to help her reveal Star Guy's true identity. I could just have told her. Zack Parker. My big brother.

"Technically," said Serge, "you cannot *unmask* Star Guy, since he does not wear *le* mask."

She tutted. "I was using it *metaforestry.*"

I was pretty sure that wasn't the right word, but this wasn't the moment to point it out.

"Don't you want to know who he really is?" she asked, studying our reactions.

"Uh . . . I . . . guess," I stuttered.

"You guess?" She looked offended.

Serge stroked his chin thoughtfully. "Personally, I am conflicted. On the one hand, *oui*, I should very much like to know the secret. But, on the other hand, to know would spoil . . . how do you say? The mystery."

Lara scowled. "What about you, Luke? Worried you'll spoil the *mystery*?"

I was more worried what would happen if Zack found out I'd helped unmask him. And why was Lara so interested? Surely she couldn't be Nemesis. For one thing, I'd heard her laugh plenty of times, and she honked like a goose. I sized her up. Sometimes in stories the villain is the very last person you expect, but this would be ridiculous.

"Why do *you* care who he is?" I quizzed her.

"It's what reporters do—investigate stuff."

Of course. Lara worked on the school newspaper. It was called *Monthly Planet*, and it had been shut down four times for spreading scurrilous rumors about various teachers. I didn't know what "scurrilous rumors" were exactly, but I guessed they were worse than regular rumors. And now Lara was sniffing out a story on Star Guy. She wasn't Nemesis, but this was bad enough.

"It'll be the scoop of the term," she breathed. "Even bigger than last year when Jill Jameson revealed the shocking truth about the local dog show."

"But why do you need us?" I asked.

"Because I had a brilliant plan, but thanks to Checkpoint Charlie over there," she thumbed at the security man on the front door, "that plan is a bust."

"What exactly was your plan?" asked Serge.

"Well, first of all, it was called Plan A," she said proudly.

"I like it," he said.

"And Plan A involved clearing the shop using a home-made stink bomb and my great-grandpa's World War II gas mask." On a hook next to the security man hung her confiscated bag. "But now Plan A is in that satchel."

Serge nodded. "So *we* are Plan B."

She took a long look at us and bunched her lip. I'd seen that look before, during PE class, whenever they picked teams and it was just me and Serge left.

And then she said, "Let's call it Plan . . . F."

She motioned us to a quiet corner of the shop, where we huddled behind a life-size cardboard cutout of three jetpack-wearing ninjas to discuss our next move.

"Have you seen the footage on the Internet of Star Guy?" she asked.

"I might have glanced at it," I said casually. I wasn't going to tell her I was *in* it.

"Did you notice Star Guy flying in to stop the bus?"

Flying? Perhaps she wasn't as smart as she thought. "No, of course not. Star Guy can't fly."

"Exactly!" She snapped her fingers. "Which means he must *already* have been close by when the bus lost control." She formed her fingers into a camera lens and closed one eye. "Judging by the angle from which the video was taken, I estimate that when he first saw the 55 coming down Main Street, he was standing at the bus stop outside this very comic book store."

She was right. Not that I was about to confirm it for her.

"And that's not all," she continued. "In the video you can see that Star Guy has something poking out of his back pocket. I've examined the footage carefully and identified what it is." She grabbed a comic from the nearest shelf and pointed at the cover. It was an issue of Savage Wolverine.

Serge looked confused. "*Wolverine* was in Star Guy's back pocket?"

I felt a prickle of unease. I knew what Lara was hinting at. "Star Guy had a comic in his pocket."

"Bingo!" She slapped me on the shoulder. It was an unexpectedly hard slap and could easily have left a bruise. "Which means he must have been in *this* shop right before he saved the day."

She was right again.

"They don't let you in here wearing a hoodie," she continued.

Crystal Comics's policy was no hoodies, no helmets,

no masks. Which I'd always thought was a bit strange, given that most of the characters in their comics wore disguises of some sort.

Lara pointed to the ceiling, where a small, black electronic eyeball swiveled at the end of a short stalk. "So my guess is he was filmed by one of these security cameras, *without* his hoodie." She concluded her brilliant deduction, and I noticed that her elf-like ears were pink at the tips with excitement. "All we have to do is watch the video from that day, and we'll see Star Guy's face."

This was a disaster. A catastrophe. A *disastrophe*! Zack and I had been in here, just as she'd said. And I had little doubt we'd been caught on video by one of the many cameras dotted throughout the shop.

I had to stop her from getting that footage.

"You have to help me get that footage," said Lara, looking right at me. "In fact, you're the key to my new plan."

Oh, no. This was getting worse by the second. "Me?" I shook my head vigorously. "No, I'm no key. Keyless, that's me. I'm not even allowed my own front door key. If I get locked out or it's an emergency, Mrs. Wilson next door has a spare, but I wouldn't like to ask her, not after dropping a hammer on her cat. Although it *was* an accident. And it's just a little limp."

Lara looked at me questioningly. "What are you talking about?"

"Keys," I said. "And you started it."

She sighed and grabbed my arm. The sore one. "Come with me."

"I . . . I can't," I stuttered. "I'm busy. I have homework."

"It'll wait," she said. "Anyway, you owe me."

"Do not."

"Do so. One word." She held up a finger. "Uni-ball Gelstick Pen with a 0.4 mm tip."

"That's not one word," I complained, but she simply smiled. She had me. If only I'd returned her stupid pen, I wouldn't be in this mess. I felt sure that in the great scheme of things, a pen—even a uni-ball Gelstick—was not worth the same as a superhero's secret identity.

The three of us took the elevator to the basement. As the doors slid shut and the theme from the ancient TV series of *Batman*—played for some reason on the pan flute—filled the small compartment, I began to sweat. How had I ended up here, helping Lara expose Star Guy? Superheroes needed secrecy. It was a well-documented fact. The only superheroes that managed to live in public were those like Iron Man, and he could only manage because he was a billionaire. Zack got an allowance, but you can't maintain a secure superhero lifestyle on six dollars and fifty cents a week.

My T-shirt was sticky with perspiration, and I could feel a fat drop of sweat roll down my forehead and tickle the end of my nose. I clung to one calming thought like it was a doughnut in shark-infested pudding: there was no way the people who owned Crystal Comics were going to let some cub reporter like Lara look through their security footage.

"I know what you're thinking," said Lara. "There's no way the people who own Crystal Comics are going to let some cub reporter like me look through their security footage. Right?"

What was it with this girl—could she read my mind?

"I . . . I wasn't thinking anything like that," I lied.

"Well, it's true. That's why we're *not* going to ask their permission."

And I thought her sister was the rebel. "Isn't that . . . breaking the law?"

"Absolutely not," said Lara. "What we're doing is called 'in the public interest.' That's what reporters say when they break the law, and that makes it OK."

It didn't sound OK. It sounded exactly like breaking the law to me.

"I have always wanted to take part in *un heist*," said Serge, seemingly unaware that Lara was leading us into the sort of trouble that ends up with phone calls to parents from stony-faced police officers.

Lara was as eager to go through with this as Serge.

"And when you get your story and it's better than anyone else's in the world—*which this is*—you win an award that you can put on your shelf. I've already cleared a space on the one in my bedroom. And from that day on you get your picture in the paper next to all the stories you write." She drew an imaginary byline in the air. "Lara Lee, award-winning reporter."

Serge nodded enthusiastically, and the two of them chattered on about prizes and fame and bedroom shelving.

Earlier that day I'd wanted so much to tell Serge the secret of Star Guy's identity. I wanted to get it off my chest. I wanted people to be impressed at what I knew. If I'm honest, a little part of me wanted to get back at Zack for being a superhero when I was not. But this was different. Lara wanted to plaster his face all over *The Monthly Planet*, and I had to stop her.

I had an idea. I would pretend to help, but what I'd really do was sabotage her efforts. I was a double agent. If I had anything to do with it, Plan F was toast. Burned toast. With lemon curd. Which I hate.

The elevator grumbled to a halt, and the doors slid open on the familiar alien landscape bathed in a sickly green glow. There was a smell of toilets.

With most people upstairs at the launch of the new Star Guy comic, there was just a handful of shoppers and even fewer red-uniformed employees down here. We made our way in single file across the mist-shrouded floor, past the pretend booby traps, skirting the pretend lava pits. The scarily calm computer voice that counted down the self-destruct sequence reached forty. I knew that when she reached zero, she'd just start again at a hundred—like she always did—but right at that moment it felt as if we really were running out of time.

"Get down!" hissed Lara.

We ducked behind a large plastic boulder. I looked at Lara. It's not as if I'm a Goody Two-shoes, but she was something else. She was wild and fearless, rushing headlong into danger like a video game character who knows that even if she slips off the edge of the cliff, it'll be OK because she'll respawn, good as new. If I'd known how much trouble she'd get me into when I borrowed her uni-ball Gelstick Pen with a 0.4 mm tip, I'd have borrowed Rupashi Singh's pencil instead.

Slowly, we peered over the boulder.

"There," said Lara, pointing at the door marked "Airlock." "That's our target."

"The staff bathroom?" I said, somewhat surprised.

"That's what they want you to think," she said, tapping a finger against the side of her nose, "but look."

I peered into the shadows off to one side of the door. There stood a figure in red, perfectly still.

"He's a watchman," said Lara. "He watches the security cameras."

"So why's he standing outside a bathroom?"

"It's not a bathroom," she snapped. "And he must be on a break."

"I think he is armed," said Serge, squinting into the gloom. "Oh, no, wait. It is not a semiautomatic machine gun with night vision laser sight. It is a meatball sub."

Easy mistake to make, I thought.

"See," said Lara, "he's on his *lunch* break. Now follow me."

She pressed her back against the wall, and we copied her, edging our way inch by inch toward the door marked "Airlock," keeping out of sight of the guard gobbling down his lunch. As we crept closer, there was a loud rumble from Serge. He held a hand to his stomach and made an apologetic face.

"Pardon," he whispered. "It is the thought of that delicious sub. It is making me hungry." His stomach gave a growl. "I cannot go on."

"Of course you can," I said. "We're not leaving you behind."

"You must. You have to." He rumbled again. "Leave me. You two must complete the mission. Do it for me. Do it for Fra—I mean America."

"Are you sure?"

"*Oui*. I will be all right." He thumbed over his shoulder. "I think I saw a Supasnax vending machine back there."

We shook hands. Serge does that a lot—it's a French thing—and then he kissed Lara on both cheeks. That's another French thing. He straightened, raised one hand in a stiff salute, and then melted away in search of a Twix. And probably a Snickers too, if I knew Serge.

The self-destruct sequence reached fifteen.

We were almost at the door. It didn't have a regular handle; instead there was a keypad.

"Oh, no. It needs a code to open it," I whispered, pretending to be disappointed, but secretly relieved. "What a pity," I groaned, hoping I wasn't overdoing it. "So near and yet so—what are you doing?"

Lara hunched over the electronic lock and began to prod at the keypad. She sounded the numbers as she hit the relevant keys. "Five . . . two . . . one . . . nine."

With a rapid series of clicks, the door swung open.

My mouth opened and closed like a surprised goldfish. "But . . . but how did you know?"

"It's the address of the shop. Five-two-one-nine Main Street." She shrugged. "Kind of obvious, don't you think?"

Before I could reply, a muffled voice pierced the darkness. "Who's there?" The watchman stepped out of the shadows, his meatball sub raised threateningly. He hadn't seen us yet, but a few more steps and he'd be on us.

"Three seconds to self-destruct," said the computer voice.

If I'm honest, I've never been all that great in a tight situation.

"Two seconds to self-destruct."

"Cool under pressure" is definitely not my middle name. I mean, it would be a pretty unusual middle name for anyone, but . . . that's not the point.

"One second to self-destruct."

Lara shoved me through the open door.

BORKEDYBORK

Lara's intelligence was correct—it was not a staff bathroom. We stood inside Crystal Comics's control room. Before you get the idea that we had stumbled on some hi-tech lair buzzing with operators peering at banks of surveillance cameras, talking into headsets saying things like, "Intruders on level forty-seven—release the Mechahounds!" you should know that a toilet would have been more impressive than the sight that greeted us.

It was a dusty, windowless room no bigger than a broom closet. Tucked against one wall were a sagging desk and a swivel chair whose best swiveling days were behind it. Flickering light came from a bulky monitor that squatted on the desk next to an ancient computer tower and a stained keyboard covered in crumbs. The monitor displayed pictures fed to it from cameras located around the store, cycling through them every few seconds. Briefly the image settled on the vending machines on the ground floor, and I glimpsed Serge contemplating his confectionery options like a cat curled around a fishbowl.

Lara swept up a crumb from the keyboard and scrutinized it with big, dark eyes. "This is bread from a sub," she concluded with a raised eyebrow. "Judging from the crumb pattern I estimate that the watchman will finish his lunch in fewer than six bites before returning to his post. A bite every thirty seconds gives us three minutes. Four with parmesan." Lara looked at me expectantly. Quite what she expected, I had no clue.

"Luke, you're up," she said, pulling out the swivel chair.

"You want me to sit in the chair?"

She made a face. "You'll be more comfortable when you hack into the security cameras."

"Hack . . . the . . . cameras?"

"Yes. Why else do you think I brought you on this mission?"

"Uh, I thought that I was a distraction. Like a stink bomb or . . . a herd of wildebeests."

"A herd?" She paused. "Of wildebeests?" She pursed her lips. "Why *wildebeests* exactly?"

"I don't know," I confessed. "It was the first thing that came into my head. I'm not sure exactly what a wildebeest even looks like. I think it might be like a cow. But with flair."

I could see from her expression that she wasn't sure if I was joking or serious. For your information, I was serious. I knew as much about wildebeests as I did about hacking. She slid the chair squeaking across the floor. I caught the headrest with one hand and, with a gulp, sat down. I squeaked back to the desk.

"You want me to hack the security system for footage of Star Guy?"

She nodded. "You're a boy. Boys know about this stuff."

"That's like saying all girls know how to bake."

She snapped the seat around so that I faced the screen, leaned into my ear, and whispered, "I have a black belt in cupcakes. Now get on with it."

I looked down blankly at the keyboard. Little did Lara realize that she had played right into my hands. Not only did I want that footage to remain hidden, I had absolutely no idea how to find it in the first place. I smiled inwardly. She had picked me for a task for which I was utterly useless. Brilliant! However, I thought I'd better play up to her expectations, so I prodded a few keys, creased my brow, and sighed a lot. Then I got a little carried away. I didn't know any actual hacker jargon, but that wasn't going to stop me. I smacked the keys in pretend frustration.

"It's no use," I said. "The Shweitzer interface on this thing is locked down tighter than the Hulk's underpants. Whoever built this rig knew what he was doing. I've got perimeter über-bots up the wazoo. And as for the borkedybork file, well it's completely . . . um . . . borked." I pushed myself away from the desk and shook my head in mock frustration. I looked up to see if Lara was buying it. She was bent over the keyboard.

"Here," she said, swiping a couple of keys and bringing up a menu. "It's the backup directory." With a shimmy of her hips she bumped me out of the chair and lowered herself in front of the monitor. Her face glowed in the screen light.

She navigated swiftly through a couple more menus and then sat up.

"This is it," she said excitedly. "Look."

She hovered the cursor over a folder dated to the day that Zack had first blazed to the rescue as Star Guy. Lara was a double-click away from revealing Star Guy's true identity. If I was going to stop her, then I had to do something now. I needed a distraction. There was never a wildebeest around when you wanted one.

"I think I hear the watchman," I whispered.

With an anxious glance at the half-open door, Lara dug into a pocket and drew out a high-capacity flash drive. She sucked the file onto the drive before tucking it securely back in her jeans.

I was going to have to get my hands on that drive.

The door swung inward. Beside me, I heard Lara let out a small gasp of horror. I held my breath, awaiting the inevitable. There was a rustle and a rasp, and then a figure stepped into the dim light of the control room.

"*Bonjour,*" breathed Serge, Ventolin in one hand, bag of salt-and-vinegar chips in the other.

Lara sighed with relief. "Let's get the heck out of here," she said, darting for the door. "That meatball sub isn't going to last forever."

IT'S NOT AN EVIL COMPUTER

Lara, Serge, and I sat together on the bus home. She chatted nonstop about the story on Star Guy she planned to write that afternoon, while I contemplated picking her pocket, but rejected that on the basis that I'm not a nimble-fingered Victorian street urchin. Serge left us at the next stop. Only two more to go before ours. I needed a miracle.

Actually, what I needed was an alien invasion.

I'd often thought that if I were an evil alien overlord I'd commence my invasion of Earth with a massive electromagnetic pulse that would neutralize every electrical device on the planet. The people of Earth would be at my mercy: planetary defenses down, power grid on the fritz, the whole world unable even to make a slice of toast. Not that making toast would be the first thing on the minds of the panicking humans as my mighty galactic mother ship disgorged atmospheric strike fighters to rain evil alien destruction across the planet, blasting strategic targets. Like my school. And the dentist.

An electromagnetic pulse would wipe the data from the drive in Lara's pocket in a nanosecond. I squinted through the window at the sky, scanning the cloud formations in hope.

"What's up?" asked Lara.

I pointed to a hulking black cloud. "Does that look like an alien mother ship to you?"

Lara fixed me with a look. "Y'know, you're even weirder than I thought," she said. But not unkindly.

Before I knew it, we were at our stop. We walked the last half mile to Moore Street and paused outside her house. I had failed in my mission, and tomorrow Zack would be splashed all over the front page of the school newspaper.

"Well, bye, then," I said, trudging off along the pavement, already figuring out how to break the awful news to Zack. Being revealed as Star Guy couldn't be good for his upcoming battle against Nemesis. If Zippy the Doorbell was telling the truth, the whole world—two whole worlds—were circling the galactic toilet bowl because of a cub reporter trying to land the story of the school year.

"Where are you going?" Lara called after me, holding up the drive. "Don't you want to see what's on this?"

A few minutes later we were in her big sister Cara's bedroom. Cara was not.

We threaded our way past balled-up clothes and discarded shoes to a desk at the window that overlooked a small backyard ringed by a wooden fence. Over it, I glimpsed our tree house, two yards away. Zack was probably alone in there right now. Either that, or he was out rescuing people and stopping criminals.

"Cara's out for the afternoon," Lara explained. "With Matthias."

"Oh, OK," I said, not really that interested.

She huffed, bothered by my lack of curiosity. "Matthias is her boyfriend. He's from Sweden. Cara says he's 'soulful.' And Mom and Dad don't know about him."

So, Cara had a secret boyfriend. I glanced again at the tree house. Zack would be crushed. But he had enough on his plate saving the world without having to hear that his dream girl was dating a sensitive Viking. I decided to keep it from him. Another secret for me to shoulder.

Lara opened the desk lid and pulled out a shiny silver laptop.

"This is Cara's," she explained, with a note of irritation. "Mom and Dad gave it to her last Christmas. And do you know what they gave me?"

"Shoes?" I guessed.

"Worse." She flipped open the laptop and mashed the

power button. "Ballet lessons," she spat. "I mean, do I look like a ballerina?"

"Maybe you will after the lessons?" I suggested.

With a glower she sat down at the computer. As we waited for it to boot up, I glanced around Cara's bedroom. I'd never been in a girl's bedroom before. Her bed didn't have flowers or ponies on the duvet cover and looked just like a normal bed. On the walls were a smattering of posters—two of a stubbly-faced singer I vaguely recognized, one of a black-and-white French film. And of course there was one of her in Star Guy's arms. Apart from that, there was a disturbing lack of superhero posters.

The home screen blossomed on the laptop, and the hard drive stopped whirring. Lara slotted in the flash drive.

"This is it, Luke," she said, her voice rising with anticipation.

Part of me wanted to tell her to relax, maybe do some yoga. I saw her glance quickly at the poster of her sister and Star Guy on the wall. It was a look I recognized at once: Lara was jealous of her big sister.

It made perfect sense. Since that day Cara had become a celebrity, and everyone wanted to be her friend. Lara, on the other hand, was forgotten. Overlooked, second best, just a nameless extra in the background. I felt the same way about Zack. The difference was that Lara had done something about it. If she could land her story, then she'd eclipse her big sister. I didn't want her to succeed, but I couldn't help but be impressed.

"Here we go," she said, the arrow hovering over the "play" icon.

Any moment now she'd discover that Star Guy was my brother. I prepared myself for the inevitable by closing my eyes and wishing I was in a galaxy far, far away. I heard the double-click of doom.

"What?! That's not possible."

Her shrill surprise gave me hope. Gingerly, I opened one eye to see her dragging the cursor back and forth over the video time line.

"It's not here," she groaned.

"What are you talking about?" I leaned on the desk for a better look.

Instead of recording the whole afternoon, the footage jumped from two o'clock straight to three, meaning the time that Zack and I were in the shop was missing. Lara banged her fist against the desk in frustration.

Relief flooded through me like an ice-cold can of Coke. Zack's secret was safe. For now.

"Maybe the cameras broke down," I suggested. "That control room wasn't exactly S.H.I.E.L.D.'s Helicarrier."

She gave me the kind of stare that would have made my head explode if she'd been an evil telepath. "The cameras stopped working at the *exact moment* Star Guy happened to be in the shop? Yeah, sure, because that's *so-o-o* likely."

Something told me that Lara's instincts were correct. It was no coincidence that the footage had vanished.

"Someone removed that hour," she said.

"Someone." I held up a finger. "Or some*thing*."

Lara shot me a doubtful look. "Uh, no. Don't think we're looking for a *thing* here, Luke. Pretty sure it's a person who did this."

I shrugged. "Could be an evil computer, or a being made entirely of energy, or—"

"Luke!"

"Yes?"

"It's a person who did this. A real, flesh-and-blood person. And he—or she—sliced out the section that reveals Star Guy's identity." She pushed the chair away from the desk and began to stalk around the room. "What we have to figure out is who and why."

I didn't say it, but of course the most likely suspect was Nemesis. This could be part of her plan to defeat Star Guy.

I couldn't put it like that to Lara without giving the game away, so I said, "Maybe whoever has the footage took it for the same reason you want it—to tell the world who Star Guy really is."

She shook her head. "If that was their aim, then they would have done it by now." She tapped a finger against her cheek. "No," she mused, "whoever did this had an *interior* motive."

"Um, do you mean *ulterior?*"

"Uh, no," she scoffed. "That's not even a word."

"OK," I conceded. It wasn't worth arguing.

"If we're going to find out *why* they did it, then the first thing we have to do is find out *who* we're dealing with. Who has access to the Crystal Comics control room?"

"What about Meatball Sub Guy?" I said.

"Yes, but he's low-level. Just a goon working for the big boss. There's always someone in the shadows pulling the strings," she said, opening a new window on the laptop and typing a subject into the search engine. "Ah-ha! Now this is interesting."

At the top of the page was a photograph of an unsmiling man who looked a few years younger than my dad. Blue eyes narrowed behind black-rimmed spectacles. A lock of dark hair curled in the middle of his high forehead. His face looked clenched, his expression that of someone who didn't want his photograph taken. The photograph went along with an article for Blam!, a well-known comic book blog.

"Christopher Talbot, owner of Crystal Comics," read

Lara. "It says here that he's a millionaire playboy and *flan-therapist*." She shook her head. "Typical rich man, wasting his money on stupid eggy pie-based treatments when there are thousands of people who need *real* medical help."

I skimmed the article over her shoulder. "It's not *flan-therapist*. It's *philanthropist*. I think it means he gives away his money to good causes."

"Oh," said Lara, disappointed.

Armed with this knowledge, we turned again to Christopher Talbot's photograph and studied him in silence. Did he look less suspicious now that we knew what he did with his riches? It was hard to say. For me. For Lara, it was less hard.

"He owns Crystal Comics, so he has access to the security camera footage. He could be the one who removed the Star Guy section." She slapped a fist into her palm. "We have to investigate him."

There was a click from the door. A dizzying waft of perfume entered the room moments ahead of its wearer. Cara stood in the doorway, blazing like the eye of Sauron.

"What are you doing in my room?!" she yelled. "You'd better not be using my laptop."

"Mom said I could," protested Lara.

I felt fairly confident that was a lie. And I was not the only one.

"No, she did not," said Cara, folding her arms and leveling her fiery gaze of doom at Lara. "Mom would never let you in here without checking with me first." She took a step toward her hapless sister. "And I haven't spoken to her since she told me I was leaving the house wearing this skirt over her dead body."

I decided to make like a hobbit and get my furry feet out of there, fast. I edged toward the door, hoping to slip out before she noticed me, but as I made my bid for freedom, I tripped over a pair of Cara's discarded sneakers and fell on my face. When I looked up she was glaring down at me. After seventeen hours of the movies, DVD extras, several average video games, a horrendously expensive role-playing game, and all three books, I finally understood how Frodo must have felt.

"You!" she spat. "You're the brother of that weird kid who stalks me at school. What are *you* doing here?"

I got unsteadily to my feet, pressed a palm to my forehead, and staggered around like a dazed fawn.

"Where . . . where am I?" I stuttered.

I wasn't actually dazed; I was pretending. "The last thing I remember was a bright light in the sky, eerie music, and then some kind of tractor beam. I . . . I think I was abducted by aliens and then teleported here." I blinked slowly at Cara.

"Another weirdo! Out," she snapped, pointing to the

door. "Both of you, out of my room. RIGHT NOW."

Lara and I hurried past her outstretched finger. The bedroom door slammed behind us. As we trotted downstairs, I thanked my lucky stars. I'd survived the day without being arrested, vaporized, or worse. Nonetheless, there was no question in my mind that Lara was a dangerous person to be around. She should be forced to wear a warning label: "Hanging out with this girl may be hazardous to your health."

She held open the front door. Safety was a few paces away. Thanking her for a *lovely* day, I scooted past, relieved to be out of there in one piece.

"Monday," Lara barked, "after school. You and I are *finally* going to unmask Star Guy."

Before I could object she had turned on her heel, and I was left staring at the closed door.

I'd squeaked through today. Monday didn't look so promising.

WITH ONE BOUND

"Her bedroom?" quizzed Zack.

"Yes."

"I don't believe you."

"Fine. Then don't."

"Her *actual* bedroom?"

It was later that evening. Zack tripped after me around the kitchen as I gathered ingredients for a milk shake. He had been going on like this for about an hour. I rolled my eyes. It wasn't as if I'd been to Superman's Fortress of Solitude or the Batcave. "I don't know what the big deal is. It's just a bedroom."

"No, no, it isn't. It's *Cara Lee's* bedroom." He stood in front of me, blocking my way. "So?"

I dodged around him and hopped up on the counter. "So, what?"

"So . . . what was it like?!" he snapped.

"Perfume-y," I said. "Oh, and she has posters of that singer. Billy-something."

"Dark?" There was a wisp of disappointment in his voice. "She likes Billy Dark?"

"That's the one. Didn't you say you hated him?"

Zack cleared his throat. "I don't think I said that I *hate* him. *Hate* is a very strong word, Luke."

I slid off the countertop, confused. "But I remember the conversation we had. We were watching that video of him with the sad giraffe and the hat. 'Can't stand him,' you said. 'With his ridiculous stubbly face, terrible songs, and stupid hat. Miserable, tuneless airhead.' Then you said that you positively, absolutely hated him. With a passion."

"Yes, well." Zack squirmed. "Maybe I was . . . hasty. Cara really likes him?"

"Two posters. Right over her bed."

"What else?"

"Nothing much." I shrugged. "Although it did get interesting when she walked in on us."

If Zack had been a cartoon character, his eyes would have been out on stalks. "She was there?!" His face flushed scarlet, much as it had that time I slipped raw chilies into his cheese and pickle sandwich.

"Did . . . did she mention me?" he asked haltingly.

I believe her exact description of him was "that weird

kid who stalks me at school." I decided to spare him the truth.

"Yes, she did," I said. "You're very memorable."

Zack's face glowed with happiness. "Memorable? She said I was *memorable*?"

Not as memorable as Matthias the Viking, I thought. But kept my mouth shut.

As Zack mooned around the kitchen mouthing "memorable" and grinning to himself, I whipped up a couple of chocolate milk shakes from my own recipe. Eight scoops vanilla ice cream. Splash of whole milk. Mini marshmallows, lightly microwaved. Plenty of whipped cream. And powdered cocoa. Not the cheap stuff—I only use Mom's really expensive Colombian chocolate powder that she keeps in the locked cupboard above the bread box. I'm not supposed to go near it, but really, can a grown-up truly appreciate a chocolate milk shake the way a kid can?

I plugged in the hand mixer and mixed up the ingredients in a large bowl. Most of the mixture stayed in the bowl, although a fair amount ended up spraying the tiled backsplash. But then, isn't that what backsplashes are for? I poured two mugs to the brim and fished out four straws from the drawer. You need two straws in each mug to maximize sucking efficiency. I handed a mug to Zack and sat down at the kitchen table.

I knew that I should tell him about Crystal Comics and the missing video footage. There was a good chance that whoever had it already knew that Zack was Star Guy. That was something he should be made aware of, if only to prepare him for the likelihood of being exposed. I was just waiting for the right moment to speak up. But somehow, ever since I'd gotten home from Lara's, the right moment had failed to present itself. I knew it was stupid, but I worried that Zack would blame me, since I was the one who had talked him into visiting the comic store in the first place.

Right then I decided that the footage was my problem, not his. I'd find it and get rid of it, and Zack would never need to know.

"So, what did you do today?" I asked him.

I could tell that he was still distracted by thoughts of Cara.

"Oh, nothing," he said with a dismissive wave. "Went to Speech & Drama this morning. Then in the afternoon stopped a runaway train."

I nodded and sucked a mouthful of milk shake. Zack had only been a superhero for a short time but was already nonchalant about the whole thing. Grown-ups are always complaining about young people having short attention spans. When you come across a fourteen-year-old boy bored of his superpowers after just a few weeks, you can't really blame them.

"Oh, yeah," he added. "Almost forgot. I discovered another new power today."

I choked on my milk shake. Now this was interesting. "X-ray vision? Energy blast? Precognition?"

"What's precognition?" asked Zack.

"It's when you can see into the future," I explained. "Not like years into the future, but seconds. And usually it's not that clear, more like a feeling in your gut, so you can sense imminent danger. Is that it, then?" I said excitedly. "I know—we'll call it 'Star-sense!'"

"No, it's not that."

"Oh," I said, disappointed. "Then what is it?"

"Well . . . I went for a swim at the sports center," he began, settling himself into the chair across from me. "It's a great pool. Huge. Fifty meters long."

I didn't care. I knew how big the pool was. But I knew, too, that if I interrupted him, this story could go on until I was old enough to leave school. I nodded and let him get on with it.

This is what I heard: "Blah blah blah. Excellent shower facilities. Blah blah blah. Delicious chicken sandwich. Blah blah blah. I can breathe underwater. Blah blah—"

"What!?" I leaped up from my seat and scampered

around the table. I stood directly behind him in order to study the back of his head.

"What are you doing?" he asked, craning his neck to see what I was up to.

I poked at his ears. "Checking for gills."

"Get off!" He pushed away my finger. "I am not a haddock!"

He was right. There were no gills behind his ears.

"That doesn't make sense," I puzzled.

Gills extract oxygen from water and then poop out carbon dioxide. It's how fish breathe. I folded my arms, baffled. "How can you breathe underwater without the correct equipment?"

"I don't know," said Zack in a bored voice. "Maybe it's magic."

I supposed it could have been magic. Plenty of super-heroes' powers had supernatural origins. Off the top of my head, I could name Hellboy, Zatanna, Constantine, and Doctor Strange.

So Zack could magically breathe underwater. I wondered how that fit into his upcoming battle against Nemesis. Maybe Nemesis would turn out to be half-shark, half-platypus or have tentacles instead of arms. Maybe the battle to decide the fate of the world would take place in the fifty-meter pool at Crystal Palace Sports

Center. That would be great for me, since I had a season pass.

Noisily, I drained my milk shake and headed out of the kitchen. It was getting late, and I had to prepare myself for Monday and another day with the hazardous Lara. I'd need plenty of sleep. I was halfway across the kitchen when a light pulsed outside the window. Looking out across the houses I saw a beam of light spearing into the sky, turning the underside of a cloud brilliant white with the giant letters "S" and "G."

"Uh, Zack?" I turned to him.

"Oh, yeah, that's for me," he said, rising from his chair. "It's new. When the Council needs me they shine that searchlight."

I gazed at the light in awe. "The Council . . . of Elrond? The Jedi Council?"

"The city council," said Zack. "The light's on the Civic Center roof."

"What if it isn't cloudy?"

"What?"

"If there are no clouds in the sky, then where do they shine the light?"

"I don't know. We didn't discuss it."

"Maybe you should bring it up at the next meeting."

"Yeah, I'll do that," he said, but in a way that told me

he had no intention of doing so. "I have to go now, Luke."

He bounded out, and I followed him into the hallway.

When I got there he was plucking his hoodie from the coat stand and pulling open the front door.

"Zack?" I called after him. "Can I come with you?"

He gave a half-amused, half-apologetic laugh. "Sorry, little brother, but this looks like a job . . ." He squared his shoulders, cloaked himself with the hoodie, and growled, ". . . for Star Guy." With that he bounded out into the night.

I hadn't noticed until that moment, but Zack barely walked anywhere these days; instead he bounded all over the place. I hurried into the driveway in time to watch him disappear along Moore Street, his swift, shadowy figure a flicker beneath the streetlights' yellow glow, as he headed off on another exciting adventure.

Without me.

BUS RIDE TO MYSTERY

Mrs. Tyrannosaur's English class was almost over. That's not, strictly speaking, her real name. We call her that because she's prehistoric, walks around with her elbows tucked in, and roars a lot.

She stood at the front of the class, waving her stubby arms and thundering on about the book we were reading. It was *The Railway Children* by E. Nesbit. A classic. If you like that sort of thing. I'd read it years ago, assuming it would be a story about a bunch of child geniuses who transform themselves into half-human, half-train cyborgs. Sort of Transformers with schedules.

It's not.

Spoiler alert. The climax of the story involves the children having to stop a train. And how do they do this, you may ask, if they have no superpowers or strength-enhancing exoskeleton suits? I'll tell you—

"Psst," a voice hissed behind me.

I turned my head to see Rupashi Singh clutching a small, folded note.

"From Lara," she whispered, thrusting it into my hand and making a kissy face.

I glanced across the classroom. I sit at the door; Lara Lee sits next to the window, as far away from me as it's possible to be. A good thing, in my opinion. Especially since I'd been trying to ignore her throughout the class. I was hoping she'd forgotten about our arrangement to meet up after school. She stabbed a finger urgently at the note. I unfolded it with a weary sigh. It was the home address of Christopher Talbot, owner of Crystal Comics and Lara's prime suspect in the case of the missing Star Guy footage. Clearly, she hadn't forgotten our rendezvous.

"Luke Parker!" roared Mrs. Tyrannosaur.

I dropped the note in alarm and blurted out, "They wave their red underpants!"

A gale of laughter billowed across the classroom. Serge laughed so hard he had to take a pull on his inhaler. Mrs. Tyrannosaur seemed less amused. The latest scientific research suggested that unlike other large carnivorous theropods the T. rex had excellent binocular vision. So did Mrs. Tyrannosaur. She eyed me beadily. Thankfully, the incriminating note had fallen into my lap, out of her sight. She lumbered over to my desk.

"To stop the train," I continued in a shaky voice, "the children wave their underpants at it." I mimed the underpant-waving action, which was probably a bit unnecessary.

Mrs. Tyrannosaur stood over me, red-varnished talons clawing the air, digestive juices dripping from her slavering jaws.

"Their *petticoats*. The children remove their red petticoats and flag down the train," she corrected. "But yes, Luke, you are substantially correct in your description of the climactic scene of the novel. I am gratified to see you were paying attention after all."

She bent down, and I could smell her breath, a mixture of rotten meat and cups of tea. Her bony nostrils flared and she snarled, "And not swapping *love letters* in my class."

I felt my cheeks burn and heard the rest of the class chuckle at my expense. All except Serge, whom I could see regarding his classmates with deep confusion. I think the French must be a lot more relaxed about all that kissy stuff.

The bell sounded for the end of the class and the school day. I had narrowly escaped the scaly clutches of my teacher, but I knew I wouldn't be so lucky with Lara Lee. There was a scraping of chairs and a clatter of shoes on the wooden floor as class was dismissed.

"OK, Romeo," whispered Lara as she breezed past me. "We have a date with Christopher Talbot."

On the bus she explained that once she'd found his address and phone number she'd called him up pretending to request an interview for the school newspaper. He'd happily agreed and invited her over for tea.

"Why did you pretend?" I asked.

Lara looked at me like I was stupid. "Because it isn't a real interview."

That seemed a shame. An interview with a comic book store owner was just the sort of thing I'd enjoy reading in the school paper. "So, if it's not a real interview, then are you going to ask him fake questions?"

"No, of course not. The questions will be real, but it's his answers I'm interested in."

"Because *they'll* be fake?"

She sighed. "His answers will tell me what he knows about the missing Star Guy footage."

That made sense, but I had one more important question. "So, who am I?"

She gave me another one of those looks. "Uh, are you feeling all right?"

"No, I mean, I know who I am *now*, here on the bus. But if you're the investigative journalist, then who am I supposed to be?"

With a smile Lara dug into her schoolbag, rummaging deep inside before emerging with a sparkly pink plastic My Little Pony disposable camera. I raised an eyebrow. "Aren't you a bit, y'know, old for . . . ?"

"I only like them ironically," she interrupted, daring me to contradict her. "You can be my photographer," she declared, handing over the camera.

I nodded. "Like Peter Parker."

"Is he your cousin?"

What?! Had she lived under a rock her whole life? No, even under-rock dwellers would know who Peter Parker was. She must have lived under a rock on the surface of the most distant rock in our solar system—which is not Pluto but actually an object called Sedna in the Oort Cloud. I mean, really, how could she never have come across the most famous newspaper photographer in the world? "He's Spider-Man."

"Oh," said Lara, offering me a mint. "Tic Tac?"

I popped one into my mouth.

"If you're going to interview a comic book store owner, you have to know the basics," I said as I crunched down on it.

She started to object, but I cut her off. "*Even* if it's a fake interview. If you don't know your Green Goblin from your Green Lantern from your Green Arrow, he'll sense that something's amiss and clam up. Then you won't find out about Star Guy."

I could see her considering what I'd said. You might think it would have been better for me to let her go into the interview unprepared. But I was in a tricky spot. I didn't want Lara to find out the truth about Star Guy, but I had to get my hands on that video footage. It pained me to admit it, but I needed her and her reporter's skills.

"We've got fourteen stops until we arrive," she said at last. "How much can you teach me about comics?"

Fourteen stops might've been enough to learn about the causes of the Civil War or a history of US presidents, but this was comic books we were talking about. "That depends. How much do you already know?"

Lara bit the end of her thumb as she pondered the question. "Well," she began, "I know that Superman can fly."

Oh. Dear.

I made a swift calculation, took a deep breath, and began. "A is for Ant-Man . . ."

TALBOT

The bus grumbled to a halt, and we hopped off. We had been stuck on "C" for the last six stops. Turns out there are a lot of superheroes called "Captain-something-or-other." I could tell by her glazed expression and the twitch in her right eye that Lara had probably heard enough about comics for now, so as we walked the rest of the way to Christopher Talbot's house she changed the subject.

"Your brother has a crush on my sister, doesn't he?" said Lara.

"I think so," I said.

Talking with girls about this stuff is a little like reading a book with Mrs. Tyrannosaur. Sometimes a sentence isn't just a sentence. Apparently, some writers put stuff into their books that you can't see. And I don't mean like DVD extras. It's called subtext. Like a submarine, it lurks under the surface. Actually, it's more like a sea monster than a submarine. A monstrous kraken. I ask you, what's the point of that? If you want people to understand your book, then why hide other meanings inside it? Comics don't have subtext. Nothing is hidden. Everything's on the outside, even the underwear. In a comic a kraken is a kraken, not a sea monster with added meaning.

"Zack's not mature enough for Cara," declared Lara.

We had some cheddar cheese in the fridge that was mature. I didn't know how that figured into this conversation so I said, "Oh."

"Matthias has a beard," she said in the same way a regular person might say, "I can teleport at will."

"A beard? Like Santa Claus?"

"Yes, Luke, just like Santa." She rolled her eyes. "No! Nothing like that. Matthias's beard is . . . what's the word?"

I sensed that I wasn't pulling my weight in this conversation, but I wanted to be helpful. "Fluffy? Furry? Fuzzy?"

"Cool," she decided.

So Cara's boyfriend Matthias was a Viking with a cool beard. I wondered what else he had going for him.

"Does he have a hammer?" I asked.

"You mean for doing odd jobs around the house?"

"No, for commanding the powers of the storm and smiting his eternal foes."

"Uh, no."

"Winged helmet?"

"Nope."

"What about a—?"

"Luke," said Lara, cutting me off. "I need to clear my head for the interview, y'know?"

"Sure."

"So, why don't we walk the rest of the way . . . in silence?"

According to the address that Lara had dug up, Christopher Talbot's house had a name: Talbot Grange. From what I knew, people who gave their houses names seldom called them Trevor or Felicity. Instead they used words like Manor, Estate, or Grange. Houses like these had stone turrets with gargoyles and butlers called Fortescue and stuffed animal heads stuck to the walls. They were set in gigantic gardens with crunchy driveways that went on for miles, and woods behind them full of stags and outlaws. So it came as something of a surprise—not to say disappointment—when we finally arrived outside Talbot Grange.

"This can't be right," I said.

We stood before an unremarkable duplex: two stories with a square bay window screened by a net curtain. The house had a driveway, but it was paved with bricks and noticeably failed to wind majestically through extensive woodland. The closest thing to a gargoyle on a turret was a one-legged pigeon wobbling on a TV satellite dish.

Lara rang the bell. Inside I could hear answering chimes playing the first bars of the theme to the 1978 *Superman* movie.

The net curtain twitched like a raised eyebrow, and a moment later the door flew open. There stood a tall man dressed all in black. It wasn't a butler, but Christopher Talbot himself. His suit shimmered like the wet hull of a Fast Attack submarine. His eyes were blue chips—not chips like you get with your lunch, the other kind. I'd seen men with eyes like his on the covers of the novels Mom liked to read. They were usually muscly hunks holding a woman in a big dress with her head tilted back. Usually they were in a desert. Or a jungle. And the hunk always had thick, wavy hair.

"Chris Talbot," he introduced himself, pushing one hand through his thick, wavy hair, offering the other to Lara. "And you must be Laura," he said, beaming at her.

"Lara," said Lara.

He noticed me standing behind her on the doorstep. "And who's your compatriot?" he asked in a friendly tone.

"I'm the photographer," I said, holding up the My Little Pony camera.

Christopher Talbot shook my hand vigorously. He

had a powerful grip, and I could feel my bones being squeezed together. "Pleased to meet you . . . ?"

"Luke," I said. "Luke Parker."

"So, Luke Parker, are you a comics fan?"

"Oh, yes. I spend all my allowance and all my birthday money at your store."

Christopher Talbot studied me carefully. "I thought you looked familiar."

He grinned, displaying two rows of toilet-bowl-white teeth. "Well, don't just stand there. Come in."

We followed him inside to a narrow entrance hall. The floor was tiled black and white like a chessboard, and his shoes made a hollow click as he led us toward a door at the end of the short hall. We stopped next to an unlit stone fireplace carved with the heads of mythological beasts. Griffins and wyverns watched us unblinkingly. A pair of basilisks looked at each other across the hearth, which was completely stupid of them, since their gaze had obviously turned them both to stone. A grandfather clock ticked in the corner. Instead of an old-timey face with Roman numerals there was an engraving of Mister Fantastic, his incredible stretched arms forming the hands of the clock. The walls were decorated with rare comics in fancy golden frames. More comics lined a flight of stairs that led to a half landing on which posed a life-size model of Iron Man.

There weren't any photos, not on the wall or on the mantelpiece over the fireplace. When you go into our house that's all you see. Dad is always making us pose for another family picture. I hate having my photograph taken, but it's very hard saying no to someone who controls your allowance. There were no photographs of Christopher Talbot and his family. Maybe he was an orphan, or maybe his family was really ugly.

"Let me take your jackets," he said.

Instead of helping us out of them, however, he tapped a code into a keypad set above the mantelpiece with his long fingers. One of the framed comics slid aside, and a mechanical arm extended from the space behind it in the wall, swaying like a cobra before dipping down to latch its metal pincers onto the collar of Lara's blazer. At least, I think it meant to grab her collar, but it missed.

"*Aow!*" she squealed, as it nipped her neck. "Get off!" She batted it away, but the coat-removing device was on some sort of automatic program. Down bobbed the snapping pincers again.

"Nothing to be concerned about," said Christopher Talbot, stabbing repeatedly at the keypad. "Just a teeny, weeny glitch." The mechanical arm froze, pincers gleaming under the hall lights. "Ah, there. Told you." With a motorized whine, it retracted into the wall. "Now, then," he said, as if the Attack of the Killer Coatrack hadn't happened, "I'll have my robot butler serve us tea in the library."

Lara gasped. "You have a *library?*"

I caught her eye. Really?

"Mr. Talbot," I piped up, "Did you say *robot* butler?"

"Indeed I did, young man. It's a hobby of mine. I designed and built him myself. In fact, I built all of the machines you see in this house."

"Even the dishwasher?" I asked.

"Well, no," admitted Christopher Talbot, "it's a Bosch. I mean I built all of the *cool* machines in the house. Like the robot butler and the auto-coatrack and the bionic toilet."

I decided immediately that if his bionic toilet worked anything like his coatrack, I wasn't going anywhere near it. I crossed my legs and tried not to think of running water.

Christopher Talbot pushed open a door and led us into the library, which was really just the living room. The walls were lined with bookcases that reached from floor to ceiling. All the books had red leather covers with their titles spelled out in gold letters. Most of them said *Reader's Digest*. A chandelier dangled like a giant earring, the fancy ones Mom wears when she and Dad go to the office Christmas party. The chandelier was far too big for the room and hung so low that we had to squeeze past in single file. Christopher Talbot motioned us to take a seat on a velvet sofa with wooden legs that ended in dragon claws. He lowered himself into a sleek armchair across from us and steepled his fingers. He watched us steadily. Lara drew out her notebook while I searched the room.

"Mr. Talbot, may I see your robot butler, please?" I asked.

A smile flickered across his face, and with a casual swipe he flipped up the arm of his chair to reveal a control unit. He reached inside for a wand-like metal rod with a bulbous black head. Some kind of microphone.

Putting his mouth to it, he cleared his throat and said, "Our guests are ready for their tea."

A hatch in one of the bookcases flew up, and out trundled his robot. To be honest, when he said he had a robot butler I had imagined something a bit more impressive—a Dalek with a bow tie, for instance, or a Sentinel with a plate of cucumber sandwiches. The thing before me was disappointingly neither.

It was about the size of a bagless vacuum cleaner, ran on tracks that appeared to have been taken from a radio control tank, and carried a silver tray on which balanced a teapot, three cups and saucers, and a plate of Oreos. Its head looked like it had been made from an old reading lamp with a flexible neck and one big flashing eye, like the Pixar logo. It juddered across the floor, causing the cups to rattle against their saucers, and came to a stuttering stop at Christopher Talbot's knee, sloshing tea from the spout of the pot.

"I call him Tal-*bot*," said Christopher Talbot proudly.

"Tea-is-served," announced Tal-bot in a halting, mechanical voice. I'd heard calculators with better speech synthesizers.

"I see you're impressed," said Christopher Talbot, cocking an eyebrow.

I didn't want to be rude, so I nodded. "Oh, yes, it's *amazing*."

"Ha!" he said delightedly. "If you think that's amazing . . ."

I didn't.

". . . wait till you see . . . this!" He lifted the microphone to his lips. "Tal-bot, engage jetpack!"

Nothing happened for a long time. Lara and I exchanged awkward glances, not sure if we should speak up.

"Tal-bot. Engage. Jetpack," repeated Christopher Talbot, his smile rigid, his forehead shiny with sweat.

"*En-gag-ing*," Tal-bot answered finally. The back cover of the robot glided open, and what looked to me suspiciously like a miniature jet engine poked out. A roar built as the engine spooled up. I didn't know much about jet propulsion beyond the basics, but even I could tell that if it really was a functioning engine, then it was far too big for the pint-size robot.

The jet roar grew, filling the room, and the air around the hot exhaust shimmered and warped. The robot shook. The tea tray vibrated, the cups, saucers, and pot inching their way to the edge before tumbling off and smashing to pieces on the floor. Christopher Talbot didn't seem to mind about the mess. My mom would have.

There was a *boom* and a blur as something shot straight up. It ripped through the glass chandelier like a Wampa ice monster brushing aside stalactites, then speared straight through the ceiling, opening a ragged hole in the floor above.

From a safe distance, behind the sofa, Lara and I gaped at the damage. Shards of chandelier glass and lumps of plaster rained to the floor. Where Tal-bot had once stood there was now only a smoking black mark, a single tread from its rubber tracks, and a scattering of cookie crumbs. I had been correct about the jet engine. It had torn free from its mountings and flown into the ceiling, its superheated exhaust gases reducing the robot butler to a smoldering blot on the rug.

Christopher Talbot hadn't moved. He sat silently in

his command chair, sporting the same fixed smile, the microphone frozen to his lips.

"Mr. Talbot, are you all right?" asked Lara, peeking out from behind the sofa.

A chunk of plaster bounced off Christopher Talbot's head, sprinkling his hair with white dust.

"Fine," he said in a quiet voice. "Now, how about that interview?"

CRYSTAL CLEAR

For a fake interview, Lara asked a lot of questions. While she quizzed him I took photos.

"The comic book business is booming," said Christopher Talbot in response to Lara's latest query. "People always need superheroes, but especially when times are hard. We all want something to believe in. So the arrival of Star Guy has been biggest thing to happen in years. The world has been wishing for a real superhero since the Golden Age of comics, and now here we have one. In our own backyard!"

Lara wrote down everything he said in a reporter's spiral-bound notebook. Her handwriting was long and loopy, like a monkey swinging through the jungle.

"The Golden Age was the 1930s and '40s," I added for her benefit. "That's when Superman first arrived from Krypton. In Action Comics, not in real life."

"That's right," said Christopher Talbot. "You know

your stuff, Luke. Very impressive. But now Superman—or Star Guy—is *really* among us. How about that?"

He was comparing Zack to Superman! OK, I had to say something. My brother might have been a superhero, but Superman was the greatest superhero of all time. Star Guy was a fourteen-year-old boy who couldn't even pee straight, if the drips on the toilet bowl were anything to go by.

"He's not really like Superman," I said.

"How so?"

"Well, for a start, he doesn't have super strength, he can't fly, and he should wear a cape," I grumbled.

Christopher Talbot laughed. "Yes, I've been thinking the same thing. If I were a superhero, I'd wear a cape *and* a mask."

"Exactly!" Frankly, it was a relief, talking to someone who understood the importance of these things.

"If Star Guy's not careful," he went on, his tone darkening, "that hoodie of his might blow off in a sudden gust of wind, and then where would he be, hmm? Exposed on the six o'clock news, that's where." He shook his head gravely.

I could tell he thought it would be a terrible thing if Star Guy's secret identity were revealed. And at that moment, looking at the concern etched on his face, I suspected I knew the truth about Christopher Talbot.

Thinking about all the gadgets in his house and his supreme love of comic books, it became clear. As clear as the Bat-Signal on a dark night. As clear as the Arc Reactor on Iron Man's chest. Crystal Comics clear.

Christopher Talbot longed to be a superhero as much as I did.

"But capeless or not," he went on, "thanks to Star Guy the interest in superheroes has never been greater. Demand for comic books is sky-high. So much that I'm opening a brand-new store next month."

I couldn't conceal my excitement. "A new Crystal Comics?"

"It will be our flagship store." He nodded. "No, our *mother ship*. Seven floors of comic book heaven."

"Is that the theme?" I asked, imagining shop assistants dressed as angels and cash registers in the shape of clouds. "Heaven?"

Christopher Talbot laughed. "Oh, no. But the theme is top secret. You'll have to wait until the store opens to find out." His face lit up as if he'd just had a great idea. "You two should come along. Yes, a couple of smart reporters ought to be at the grand opening." He looked at me. "Not to mention there's a prize drawing for a copy of Action Comics number 232 in 'fine' condition, with a Mylar sleeve, rust-free staples, minimal stress lines, no tears, and a smidgeon of a spine roll."

I gasped.

"I'll have my people arrange a couple of VIP passes." He swept back a lick of hair. "Just give me your addresses before you leave today."

A VIP pass to the grand opening of the new Crystal Comics and a chance to win my very own copy of a Golden Age comic book? I could hardly believe my luck. I was about to say thank you when Lara flicked a page of her reporter's notepad and loudly cleared her throat.

"So, Mr. Talbot, with so many customers whizzing through your doors and such valuable comics on display," she said, tapping her pen against the page, "crime must be a constant worry."

"Not with all those *crime*-fighters between the pages," Christopher Talbot said, grinning.

"But you must have excellent security," she pressed him. "I mean, video cameras and whatnot."

"Oh, I wouldn't know," he said with a dismissive wave. "I leave all that stuff to my chief executive."

Lara and I exchanged glances. So Christopher Talbot didn't know about the footage, but his chief executive might.

"Yes," he went on, "I'm interested in the strategic business. Looking to the long-term and all that. I leave the day-to-day running of Crystal Comics in the hands of—"

Just then his pocket buzzed, and a ringtone that

sounded like the theme song to the old *X-Men* cartoon series blared out. I couldn't believe it. Just as he was about to reveal the identity of—

"Walter Go," said Christopher Talbot, fishing out his phone. "I leave all that stuff in the very capable hands of Walter Edmund Go." He studied the screen. "Ah, speak of the devil!" He swiped a finger across the screen and brought the phone to his ear. "Walter, I was just singing your praises." He smiled at Lara and me. "But I'll have to call you back. I'm in the middle of a very important interview. *Ciao*." He ended the call and settled back in his chair. "Now, where were we?"

Lara asked a few more questions and then drew the interview to a close. We still didn't know who had the Star Guy footage, but we had a very good lead. Walter Edmund Go, chief executive of Crystal Comics, was our new prime suspect. We thanked Christopher Talbot for his time, and he showed us out past the wreckage of Tal-bot. Once in the hallway Lara cast a wary eye at the lurking auto-coatrack.

"Great to meet you both," Christopher Talbot said as he opened the front door. "Oh, don't forget to give me those addresses for the VIP invitations." He shoved a notebook under our noses. I scribbled my address and passed it to Lara. "Wonderful. I'll have my assistant fire those right out to you. And please send me a copy of the finished article."

We agreed that we would. Lara paused in the doorway. "I was wondering, Mr. Talbot," she said. "The interview was really good, but perhaps it would be even better with another perspiration."

Christopher Talbot looked confused, which was understandable. Lara used words the way the Hulk opened a bag of chips. You were never sure if you were going to end up with a whole chip or a handful of crumbs that looked a bit like a chip.

"Another *perspiration?*" he asked doubtfully, and then a light came on. "Oh, you mean *perspective?*"

"Yes," said Lara firmly, "that's what I said. So, I was thinking that I should interview your chief executive too. What do you say?"

Christopher Talbot brushed a hand through his hair. A lump of ceiling plaster fell out and hit the floor with a wet thud. "I say that's a terrific idea."

KRYPTONITE

I left Lara outside her house and hurried the short distance home. I'd told Mom and Dad that I was going to Serge's right after school and I'd be back for dinner. I didn't want to rouse their suspicion by showing up late.

"You look guilty," said Mom the moment I swung through the door into the kitchen. She was sitting down, fiddling with her phone. Behind her on the stove an enormous pot bubbled like an overheating nuclear reactor. She peered at me. "What have you been up to?"

Mom could always tell when I'd been up to something I shouldn't. Having discussed it with Serge, it turns out that his *maman* can always see right through him too. It's like X-ray vision for moms.

"I've been taking photographs for the school newspaper," I said. Which was true. OK, I didn't mention the part where I rode the bus to another part of town and went to Christopher Talbot's house without permission. But then, she hadn't asked.

She lowered the phone. "You? Taking part in an extra-curricular activity that doesn't involve superheroes?" She sounded doubtful.

"I'm broadening my horizons," I said, squirting dish-washing soap over my hands and running them under the tap.

"Is that so?" she said, studying me in detail, the way she checks all over to see if a pineapple is ripe in the supermarket.

Just then the back door flew open. Dad and Zack ran in from the yard, sheltering beneath a newspaper from a sudden downpour. Judging by the oil stains on their sleeves and smeared across their faces, they'd been in the shed working on the plate rack. What could oil stains possibly have to do with constructing a plate rack? Don't ask.

"That rain is *biblical*," said Dad.

"You mean it's raining frogs?" I said.

"No, what I mean is—"

"—it's rain, but wrapped in a pillar of fire," I suggested.

Dad shot a look at Mom. She shrugged. "He's your son too."

Our weather is always wonky, but lately it had

been even odder than usual. No actual rain of frogs, or cats and dogs, unfortunately, but hailstones the size of Mini Coopers, clouds as thick as pudding, and electrical thunderstorms violent enough to bring Dr. Frankenstein's monster to life.

"Good day at school?" Dad asked, ruffling my hair.

"He's working on the school newspaper now," said Mom, without taking her eyes off me.

"No, he's not," said Zack, making a face.

"Yes, I am!" I glared at him. I'd been keeping his secret for ages. Couldn't he see that it was time to repay the favor?

Mom leaned in, running her eyes over me like a laser scanner. "There's something you're not telling me, isn't there?"

There were a bunch of things I wasn't telling her. Which one did she have in mind? If I told a barefaced lie, she'd see right through me. I had to give her the truth. Sort of. "Um, you know how I said I went to Serge's after school? Well, I didn't."

"Luke Alfred Parker!" said Mom in a voice that would drown out Black Bolt's sonic scream.

She stood up, her chair scraping across the floor like talons on a blackboard.

I looked from her to Dad. Their eyes blazed with a

mixture of disappointment and displeasure. Zack stood at the open fridge, drinking straight out of an orange juice carton and chuckling at the jam I'd got myself into. Not the strawberry jam, which we don't keep in the fridge or it turns solid and doesn't spread on your toast. The other kind, when you're hanging off the edge of a cliff in the last panel of the story.

"I'm going out with Lara Lee," I said.

There was a cough and a snort as orange juice spurted out of both of Zack's nostrils. It was quite impressive.

Mom and Dad had different reactions to my confession. Dad's chin stuck out, this weird expression came over his face, and he began to nod. I'd almost say he looked impressed. Mom, on the other hand, sat down heavily in her chair again.

"My little boy's growing up," she sighed.

Mission accomplished! I had successfully distracted them from asking awkward questions about what I'd really been up to. I mean, Lara and I had *gone out* to meet Christopher Talbot, so that was a kind of "going out," right?

"He's making it up," said Zack, his lip quivering.

He turned to me, eyes wide and glistening, orange juice leaking from his nose. If I hadn't known he was a superhero, I'd have said he was about to burst into tears. "There is no way you're going out with anyone."

At that moment the phone rang and Mom picked it up. She said "hello" and then "oh" and, with a startled expression, handed me the receiver. "It's . . . Lara."

Zack made a noise like he was choking on a nut and marched out of the kitchen in a hiccuping fury. From outside in the hallway came a strangled cry of "*No-o-o!*"

I couldn't understand why he was making such a fuss. I put the phone to my ear. "Hi, Lara."

"No time for chitchat. Meet me in your tree house in five minutes."

"Does it have to be five minutes? I haven't had my dinner yet."

There was a sigh from the other end of the line. "Fine," she grumbled. "After dinner, then." She paused. "What are you having?"

I glanced at the pot bubbling on the stove. The lid rattled and clanked, and steam leaked from the gaps in white coughs. "Not sure," I said, "but I think it's trying to escape."

"Hey, I heard that," said Mom.

I cupped the phone and turned away.

"Oh, and if anyone asks," I whispered into the receiver, "we're going out."

"We're *what?*"

"I was in a tight spot. I had to say something."

"So you said I was your girlfriend?"

"Yes, but only as a diversionary tactic. So, less a girl-friend, more a wildebeest."

"What is it with you and wildebeests?" she muttered and hung up.

As soon as I'd finished dinner I headed upstairs, loudly announcing my intention to do my homework. My actual plan was to circle back and meet Lara in the tree house, but I figured I ought to make it appear as if I was going through my normal routine.

I could hear Mom and Dad downstairs, doing the dishes and dancing around the kitchen. They do that a lot, even though they're terrible dancers. At least they only do it in the kitchen and not in public where actual people could point at them. As they clomped around below, I padded across the landing, skirted the potted plant, and eased past Zack's bedroom door. He hadn't come down for dinner, and to my surprise Mom hadn't insisted. I tipped open my own bedroom door and went inside. No sooner had I stepped over the threshold than I felt a steely grip around my arm, and I was yanked the rest of the way into the room.

Zack slammed the door and turned to me.

"You can't be going out with Lara Lee," he hissed.

"Why not?"

"Because . . . because," he stuttered, shaking with fury. I felt drops of water spatter against my cheek and noticed that his hair was soaking wet. "Because I want to go out with her big sister and . . . and . . . I haven't had a girlfriend yet . . . and you're my little brother and—" his voice rose to a wail— "and it's just not right!"

He released his grip, and I rubbed my arm. I should have told him the truth. There and then I should have said, "Relax, bro. I made up the whole thing about Lara just to put Mom and Dad off the scent." But I didn't. Standing there in front of Zack, for the first time since he became Star Guy, I felt powerful. I had something that he wanted, and all I could think was: serves him right. Now he knows how it feels. A part of me knew that I was behaving badly, but another part wallowed like a pig in a mud bath at Zack's unhappiness.

"Well, we *are* going out," I said. "Lara's my girlfriend."

That shook him, but I could see he was about to probe further, and if I didn't end this conversation, he'd figure out I was lying. I knew what would shut him up. It was the nuclear option, but he had left me no other choice.

I took a deep breath and said, "She kissed me."

It was another lie, of course, but Zack stumbled like he'd been zapped by a trip ray. "You kissed?" he howled. "You're barely eleven, and you've kissed a girl. This is . . . I don't even know what this is anymore. I don't feel well," he said, flopping down on my bed.

It was true—he looked pale. The top buttons of his shirt were undone, and I could see that the star pattern on his chest, which usually shone as bright as a night-light and pulsed like a lion's heart, was dim and thready. I felt a pang of guilt. Had I done this to him with my lies about Lara? Was this Star Guy's Kryptonite?

"Zack, your stars . . ."

"I know. It happened last night," he said, rolling over and staring mistily out of the window. "I'd just prevented a bank robbery." He coughed. "Usually I feel great foiling a robbery, but yesterday I was so tired I almost let one of the robbers get away. It was a close call."

"But you didn't," I said, trying to reassure him. "You caught the bad guys in the nick of time. That's what superheroes do. They're hardly ever early."

"I haven't gotten to the worst part yet." He flipped onto his back again and stared at the ceiling. "After I handed the robbers over to the police, I was waiting for the bus and I felt it go."

"Felt what go?"

"My force field. It died. Just as I was getting on the number 43. Went out like a power cut and hasn't come back since." He circled a finger about his head. "And now my radar is down, and I just dunked my head in the bathtub to see if I can still breathe underwater."

That explained his wet hair. "And what happened?"

"I almost drowned," he said, his voice breaking.

This was bad. "But you've still got your telekinesis, right?"

"I . . . I don't know."

"Well, try it out. Start with something easy." I pointed to the lamp by the side of my bed. "Use your power to switch it on."

"OK, I'll give it a try." Zack propped himself up on the bed, flung out a hand, splayed his fingers, and leveled his gaze at the lamp. His arm began to shake with the effort. He gritted his teeth so hard they began to squeak. The bulging blue vein at his temple looked ready to pop. Then with a gasp he lowered his arm and fell back onto the bed.

"It's no use," he said with a hopeless sigh. "I've lost all my powers. How am I going to save two universes now?"

My head whirled with possibilities. Could it be? Had Zack's reign as Star Guy come to an end so soon? I'm ashamed to admit it, but a part of me was pleased. Zack had never properly appreciated being a superhero and, in my opinion, didn't deserve his powers. OK, sure, he went out and fought crime, but I could tell his heart wasn't in it and that he'd rather be in his room doing his homework.

Of course superheroes lose their powers all the time

(not that Zack would know, never having read a comic). For a while Superman gave up his powers to be human so he could go out with Lois Lane. Imagine giving up your superpowers for a girl?! And Spider-Man, Thor, and Wolverine had lost their powers too. But all of their powers came back. I was sure that Zack's would too. After all, Abzorbo the Divider gave him superpowers so he could battle Nemesis, and their climactic showdown had yet to happen.

I was about to reassure him when he turned onto his side and moaned, "There's a parents' evening at school next Tuesday."

I really shouldn't have been surprised. This was exactly the sort of thing that would be bothering him at a time like this.

"All the time I've been spending as Star Guy saving people and foiling crimes, I've been neglecting my homework." Zack swallowed hard. "My grades are slipping." His voice broke. "I'm failing math."

Before he was a superhero, Zack had been a superstudent. It seemed you couldn't be both. I knew how seriously he took his studies; he wanted to be a doctor one day, and to do that you had to get all A's from the age of three. Also, no force field in the galaxy would stop Mom and Dad's wrath when they found out he was failing math.

I was about to say something to encourage him when he let out another moan. "I feel weak. I feel ordinary. I feel useless. I feel like . . ." He lifted his eyes to look at me, and I knew what he was thinking.

He felt like me.

In that moment all my sympathy for him went up in flames. I hated my brother. I hated him with all the fury of an exploding sun. I knew that my life would be better if he didn't exist. My parents would have no one to compare me to. My report cards would never be second-best again. In our kitchen there are marks on the wall where Dad records our heights. Zack's always been taller than me, even at one year old. I've been failing to measure up to him my whole life.

"Remember when I told you Cara said you were memorable?" I said.

"Yes?"

"That's not all she said."

Zack seemed momentarily revived. He shuffled to the edge of the bed. "Tell me."

I felt strangely calm. As cold as Mr. Freeze. As remorseless as Lex Luthor. "She called you that weird kid who stalks her at school."

Zack's face sagged, and he swallowed hard. I went on, as unstoppable as Juggernaut. As deadly as Bullseye.

"And she's got a boyfriend. His name's Matthias, and he has a beard."

Zack said nothing, just slipped off the bed and trudged out of my room. He didn't even slam the door.

And as it clicked shut behind him, I knew that I had defeated Star Guy.

19

SMASH AND GRAB

I waited until Mom had gone next door to check on old Mrs. Wilson and Dad had retreated to his shed for another round with the plate rack before sneaking out to join Lara in the tree house. The air was still, the night sky hidden behind a thick bank of clouds as it had been all week. Lara wanted to discuss our next move, but I didn't care about the investigation anymore. I didn't care who knew about Zack's stupid secret identity. I was mad at him. I put a foot on the bottom rung of the rope ladder and started to climb.

I decided to tell Lara the truth about Star Guy. Let her write what she liked.

I found her sitting cross-legged on the floor beside a stack of my comics, flicking through a copy of Uncanny X-Men. She set it aside.

"I called Crystal Comics's headquarters," she said as I sat down beside her. "Walter Edmund Go can't do the interview because he's on vacation in Slovakia. Don't you think that's weird?"

"Slovakia is *quite* an unusual place to go on vacation," I agreed.

"And when I googled him, nothing came up."

"He's the Invisible Man," I muttered.

Under other circumstances that would have been cool, but right now it meant our only lead was a dead end.

"I think Christopher Talbot sent us on a wild moose chase."

"I think it's a *goose* chase."

She wrinkled her nose. "A moose is much trickier to catch than a goose. Anyway, I don't trust him. That creepy coat-strangling gadget and the exploding robot." She shivered. "Normal people don't own things like that."

I thought his auto-coatrack was cool, and there was no gadget I wanted more than my own personal robot, except perhaps my own personal jetpack.

"Did you notice there were no photographs in his house?" she asked.

I had noticed and thought it strange too, but I certainly wasn't about to admit that to her now. She would only seize on it as proof she was right to call Christopher Talbot weird. He wasn't weird—he was like me.

"I think there's more to him than meets the eye," said Lara, narrowing her own eyes.

"Well, I disagree. Just because he loves comics and lives in the house of the future doesn't make him an oddball. You could say that about most superheroes. There's more to *them* than meets the eye."

"You're saying Christopher Talbot is a superhero?" Her face lit up. "What if *he's* Star Guy?!"

It was time for the truth. "Lara, there's something I have to tell you." I took a deep breath. "My brother is . . ." I tried to get the words out. I could see them in my head, but they just sat there with their arms folded, refusing to budge. "What I'm trying to say is . . . my brother . . . Zack . . ." I knew where Star Guy's force field had gone—it was between my tongue and my brain. "Zack is . . ."

From outside came a splintering crash and the ring of breaking glass.

"What was that?" asked Lara, dashing to the door.

We peered out across the dark yard, searching for the source of the noise. There was a light on in Dad's shed and the sound of banging. He was wrestling with the plate rack, but the noise hadn't come from there, and the commotion hadn't disturbed him. I swung around to examine our house. Lights shone from the upstairs windows. They were on in the landing and in Zack's bedroom. I could see him moving around.

He hauled himself from his bed and half stumbled toward the door, but as he got there, it flew open, striking him on the shoulder, sending him spinning to the floor. Beside me I heard Lara gasp. She'd seen it too.

Extending a shaking finger to point, she said, "Luke, there's a robot in your house!"

There in the doorway of Zack's bedroom stood a giant, shining figure. As we watched, it ducked its chrome head and turned a pair of broad, gleaming shoulders sideways to squeeze through the gap. It made its way purposefully into the room, putting one hulking foot in front of the other like it was stamping on ants.

"That's no robot," I said. "It's someone in a powered suit."

Its movements were jerky, as if the suit had come right out of the box and the user hadn't yet read the manual. It headed straight for Zack. He lay on the floor, dazed by the collision with the smashed door. The figure in the powered suit was almost on top of him. I had to do something. Lara was one step ahead of me.

"Well, come on, what are you waiting for?" She launched herself over the edge of the tree house deck and shimmied down the rope ladder. I climbed after her. By the time I reached the ground, she was already easing open the back door. I caught up with her as she snuck into the kitchen. The lights were off.

"What's the plan?" I whispered in the darkness.

"We're going to stop the robot," she said, as if I'd

asked her what color was the sky. "We have the element of surprise."

She needed a reality check. "Uh, we're in here with a villain wearing a powered suit that's almost certainly designed to boost its wearer's strength, speed, and stamina, making them capable of ripping off our arms as easily as you or I would tear off a square of toilet paper, and you think that *we* have the element of surprise?"

"If you're scared, then stay here," Lara said, padding into the hallway.

"I'm not scared," I said, sticking out my jaw and following her.

We crept into the silent and dark hall. The front door hung awkwardly from one hinge, like a climber clinging to a mountain by his fingertips. The colored glass panel that formed the top section lay in jagged pieces on the carpet. Next to it, the hall table wobbled. I spotted a black coil wrapped around its legs and knelt down for a better look.

Plugged into the wall socket beneath the table was what looked like a hose from a vacuum cleaner. Something tugged on the hose, causing the table to sway. I traced its path, which snaked along the carpet out past the demolished front door.

"I have a bad feeling about this," I muttered.

I ran into the driveway only to see the back of the

powered suit as its wearer pounded across the street. The hose wound its way out along the driveway and into a socket located on the back of the metal suit.

There was a sound, faint but audible. A computerized voice warbled out of the suit. Some kind of onboard, tactical, battle computer interface, I presumed. The voice uttered a command: "At the end of the driveway, make a slight left. You have arrived at your destination."

The figure stomped toward a parked car, a minivan with blacked-out windows and no license plates. It was only as the figure paused to search the powered suit for its car keys that I saw my brother, semiconscious, held in its massive, hydraulically boosted arms.

"Zack!" I shouted.

The figure turned at my voice. For a second we locked eyes across the street. From behind its metal mask, two pinpoints glowed red. Some kind of laser range finder or infrared vision, I guessed. The figure opened the minivan door and easily tossed Zack inside.

"How do we stop it?!" yelled Lara.

Half an hour ago I'd been so angry at Zack that if someone had offered to arrange for him to be kidnapped by a supervillain in a powered exoskeleton, I would have bitten their augmented hand off. But when it happened in real life, I felt differently.

"I'm on it," I said, running back into the hallway.

I dropped to my knees and slid along the carpet. Ducking beneath the table I yanked the power cable from the socket. I heard Lara's shout. "It's stopped moving. Hurry!"

I leaped up and bolted out of the house to save Zack.

In the road the figure stood like a statue, crippled just as it was climbing into the minivan, one cybernetic gloved hand clamped to the doorframe, one leg poised above the sill. But not for long. There was a hum as it rebooted under an onboard battery pack.

The suit whirred back to life, and as we rushed toward it, the figure wedged itself into the driver's seat and fired the ignition. We were too late. The minivan pulled away with a crunch of gears. Without thinking, I ran into the road to block its path. As I faced it down, I realized it wasn't going to stop.

My legs were knocked from under me, and I felt the breath go out of my body. I lay by the side of the road and looked up to see Lara lying on top of me. The minivan hadn't struck me—she had, tackling me out of the path of the car.

We untangled ourselves and caught our breath, helpless as we watched the car disappear along Moore Street. The weight of the suit too much for the chassis, it bottomed out, leaving a trail of sparks along the road like the afterburner of a fighter jet. With a complaining squeal of tires, the car turned the corner and disappeared from sight. For a second or two the silver sparks glowed in the night air, and then as they hit cold asphalt, sizzled and went out.

"We have to call the police," said Lara, leaping to her feet.

"No. Wait." I couldn't let her do that. The police would ask too many questions. It was all happening too fast—I needed time to think.

"But your brother's been kidnapped! By a . . . by a . . . what was that thing?"

"Not what," I said. "*Who*."

I had no doubt. She had chosen her moment perfectly. She had kept out of the headlines, lurking in the shadows waiting for Star Guy to be at his weakest.

"That," I said, "was Nemesis."

YOU'RE MY ONLY HOPE

"Who's Nemesis?" asked Lara.

"No one," I said hastily.

Lara stood with a hand on one hip, wearing an expression I had once observed on my PE teacher's face just after I'd informed her that I couldn't possibly participate in that afternoon's dodgeball tournament due to an old bullfighting injury.

I started to walk back toward the house, hoping she wouldn't follow.

"Luke?" My mom stood in the gaping doorway, trying to figure out why her front door was lying in the hallway, smashed to pieces. "What happened here?"

"A supervillain in a futuristic exoskeleton abducted your firstborn who, by the way, is not just a regular schoolboy, but in fact the internationally famous superhero known as Star Guy . . ."

. . . Is what I *didn't* say.

Part of me wanted to tell her the truth. Tell her about Zack and Star Guy and Nemesis. Tell her to call the police, the army, the Justice League. But what could the police do? Nemesis was a supervillain. In comics the police are always hopeless when faced with technologically superior evil. And forget about the army—they shoot first, and their weapons are always useless. And I couldn't call on the Justice League because, well, to the best of my knowledge they weren't real. The only actual superhero in the world was my brother. And telling Mom would take away the last power he still had—his secret identity.

I looked into her questioning face and struggled to come up with an answer. The longer I hesitated, the more I could see her suspicion grow. I had to say something. Something simple. Something believable. Something fast.

"It was a gust of wind," said Lara.

Something like that.

"Yes! That's it. Wind." I jumped in, adding a great whooshing noise for effect. "*Whoooshhh . . . whoooshhh . . .*"

"Yes, Luke, I think your mom knows what wind sounds like."

Mom appeared to consider Lara's explanation.

"Well," she said at last, "there *has* been a lot of strange weather recently."

It was true; storm-force winds tearing up trees fol-lowed by eerily calm, cloud-filled days like the last few.

"Yes, very strange," I agreed, nodding far too enthu-siastically.

"Just as long as the two of you are all right." Mom gathered Lara and me to her in a huge hug, her concern for the broken door replaced by motherly concern.

"We're fine, thanks, Mrs. Parker," mumbled Lara from somewhere inside Mom's jacket.

"Where's Zack?" asked Mom.

Uh-oh.

"You know him," I said. "Nothing disturbs him when he's doing his homework."

Well, apart from being kidnapped by a supervillain.

Mom nodded. "I'd better clean this up before some-one has an accident," she said, picking her way across the glass-strewn hall to the cupboard under the stairs. As she rummaged inside for a dustpan and brush, she called over her shoulder. "Lara, it's late. I think you should be going home."

"Yes, Mrs. Parker."

"I'll walk you," I said. There was something I needed to say to her. In private.

"All right," Mom said. "But come right back." She peeled off the vacuum hose and waved it in our direction. "And no canoodling until you're twenty-one."

Lara steered me through the doorway. I wasn't sure which hit me hardest, the cold night air or the words that she hissed in my ear: "You're going to tell me everything. Right now. Or I'm going to march back in there, inform your mom that there was no gust of wind, and tell her exactly what happened tonight."

Could have been worse. She could have wanted to canoodle.

I took a moment to organize my thoughts. What I was about to do would change everything. The fact was that Nemesis had kidnapped Zack, and it was only a matter of time before my parents realized their eldest son was not in his bedroom doing his geography homework. They'd call his friends, and when he didn't show up after that, they'd contact the police. There would be tears, an anxious wait, maybe even a TV appeal for information, ending with a heartfelt plea for him to come back home. Only I knew he wasn't coming back. Without his superpowers, he was too weak to fight a cold, let alone a supervillain. He was just Zack Ravilious Parker, gold medal winner for do-goodery, the most annoying big brother ever to walk the earth.

He needed my help. And I needed Lara's.

She was smart and fearless, and she'd demonstrated her quick thinking already tonight by pulling out that explanation about the freak gust of wind. Sure, she wanted to reveal Star Guy's true identity, but if anyone could help me rescue my brother it was Lara Lee.

"Zack is Star Guy," I said.

In comics when a superhero reveals his secret identity, no one believes him at first. So I knew what Lara would say next. She'd splutter something about that being impossible, ridiculous, completely un—

"I know," she said.

"You . . . what . . . *urr* . . . how?"

She drew a hand from her jeans pocket and slowly opened her palm.

S. G.

Star Guy's sigil glittered under the streetlight. The one I'd made for him by gluing old Christmas decorations to one of Mom's brooches. It had become one of the most photographed symbols in the world, recognizable to anyone who followed my brother's exploits.

"I found it on the street," she explained. "Where the car was parked. It must have fallen off when—what did you call it? Nemesis?—bundled him into the backseat." She narrowed her eyes. "I always wondered how Zack managed to rescue Cara's phone from that drain—now I know. Telekinesis. But that's all I know. And I want the whole story. Spill it," she barked. "From the top. Page one. Go."

For the next five minutes Lara listened as I filled her

in about Zorbon the Decider bestowing Zack with super-powers. How Nemesis threatened two universes, and only Star Guy could stop her. How he'd lost his powers. How Zack refused to wear the cape I'd made him from the curtain in the downstairs bathroom. You know, just the important stuff.

When I'd finished I looked her straight in the eye and said, "I need your help to rescue him."

She displayed a knowing smile that wasn't exactly reassuring and said, "You can count on me." With a sweep of her arm she drew an imaginary headline in the night air, declaring, "Girl Reporter *Saves* Star Guy. Now *that's* a story." She rose slowly onto the tiptoes of her sneakers. It's possible she was levitating with excitement.

But before I could reply, something strange happened.

"Luke, it's me," said Zack.

"Zack?!" I spun around at the sound of his voice, expecting to see him standing there. But the street was empty.

"Luke, are you there? Can you hear me?"

It was definitely his voice, but he was nowhere to be seen.

"It's him, isn't it?" said Lara. "Is he communicating with you through telepathy?"

Telepathy: mind-to-mind communication. Zack's voice was in my head, projected by what must be the fifth of his superpowers to reveal itself. But hadn't he lost all of his powers?

"Zack" I formed the words in my head. "I can hear you. Your powers are back!"

"No, they're not. I think this is like an emergency beacon, activated in times of distress. I don't know how long it's going to last. Luke, I'm in terrible trouble."

"I know. I watched Nemesis kidnap you. There was nothing I could do to stop her."

"Ask him what he can see," said Lara. "If he recognizes a landmark, then we'll be able to narrow the search area. Otherwise it'll be like looking for a noodle in a haystack."

She was right. Not about the noodle, but definitely about tracking down Zack.

"Where are you?" I said in my head.

"Tied up in a car," said Zack.

"Can you see anything?"

"Nothing. I'm lying across the backseat."

"You have to tell me what you can see. Something memorable. A landmark."

"Good thinking. I'll try to wriggle to the window."

I glanced at Lara—seemed she was full of good ideas.

"Y'know, sometimes I wish I'd been the one who'd gone to pee that night." He sighed. "Zorbon the Decider picked the wrong brother."

I'd been thinking that for weeks, but at that moment

I realized it wasn't true. Zack had sacrificed the thing he loved (OK, it was homework, and that was weird, but whatever) in order to fulfill his responsibilities as Star Guy. He hadn't asked to be a superhero, but even so he had taken on the job, if not the mask and cape. I felt closer to my big brother than I had in years, which was upside down and back to front, since right then he was as far away from me as he'd ever been.

I experienced a strange telescoping sensation, as if I was standing at the peak of the tallest mountain in the world and all the stars in the night sky were rushing away from me. I realized I might never see Zack again. I wanted to tell him that everything would be all right, but I didn't know if it would be. Star Guy was powerless, and I was just an ordinary boy up against the sinister scheming of a super-criminal. I didn't even have a secret weapon.

"Wait, the car's slowing down . . ." said Zack.

All went quiet. "Zack?"

"Still here. We've stopped. I can lift my head a little. I might be able to . . ." There was a pause. "No way. That's impossible. There's no such thing."

"What? What is it?"

There was the sound of the car door opening and Zack being lifted out.

"We're going inside," he said.

"Inside what, Zack?" I said in my head, and then in desperation repeated it out loud. "You're going inside what?"

"I can hear voices . . . They're taking me to the . . . crater level."

"The crater level? What does that mean? Crater level of what?'

He answered through a crackle of static, and then the telepathic connection died and all I could hear were my own thoughts swirling madly inside my head.

Lara looked at me expectantly. "Well? What did he say?"

I couldn't be one hundred percent certain since the connection had been lost at the crucial moment, but I was pretty sure I'd heard him correctly.

"Luke, where is Zack being held?" demanded Lara.

I blinked and met her gaze. "A volcano."

AND THEN THERE WERE THREE

When Zack failed to appear for breakfast the following morning, Mom and Dad immediately knew that something was wrong. Zack and his Cheerios were never separated willingly. Mom knocked on his door, and when there was no answering teenage groan she went in to find that his bed hadn't been slept in. I felt bad keeping what I knew from my parents, but it's not as if hearing the truth would have made them feel any better. As I'd predicted, following a round of increasingly frantic phone calls to Zack's friends, Dad called the police.

In no time at all a policeman and policewoman showed up on our doorstep, removing their caps and speaking in soft voices. First they took statements from Mom and Dad, and then it was my turn. I knew it was bad when they sat me down on the sofa with a can of Mountain Dew and a plate of Chips Ahoy!, neither of which I'm usually allowed near unless I've first eaten my own weight in salad.

I answered their questions as best as I could. Had Zack met anyone unusual recently? Yes, a transdimensional being sent by the High Council, oh, and a supervillain called Nemesis. Had he been behaving oddly? Well, he's been running into burning buildings, holding up collapsing bridges, and generally saving people. So no, not unusual at all—*for a superhero*. Of course, I didn't say any of that out loud. I gave them bland answers that wouldn't freak them out—or get me locked up in an institution for crazy younger brothers.

When the interview was over, I told Mom and Dad that I wanted to go to school. They seemed surprised. Was I sure? If, under the circumstances, I wanted to take the day off, they'd understand. I nodded my head firmly. I was sure—I had important business to take care of. Both of them insisted on driving me right up to the school steps. Mom would have held my hand and walked me into class if I hadn't stopped her. I gave them each a hug and said I was sure Zack would be home before we knew it. Which he would, if I had anything to do with it.

After that, Zack was officially a missing child, which seemed strange to me. The police had checked the wrong box on their paperwork. He was a missing superhero. But only I knew that.

Correction: I knew, and Lara Lee knew. And before the day was out, I would have to let one more person in on the secret.

Children milled around the playground, blissfully unaware that as sporty boys kicked soccer balls and big kids kicked little kids, the meeting that was taking place on the far side of the basketball court could well decide the fate of two universes. The time was half past eleven—or Zero Bark Thirty as we called it, owing to the springer spaniel that lived in one of the houses across from the school gates and jumped up and down in the window barking its head off every morning at recess. Lara arrived on the dot, and Serge showed up moments later. He was unaware of the incredible events of last night—but all that was about to change.

"Bonjour, Lara. It is *dee-lightful* to see you once again." He pressed his lips to the back of her hand and then took a pull on his inhaler.

Why did we need Serge? It was simple. Although, like an answer to one of Mrs. Tyrannosaur's fiendish book quizzes, it was also an answer in two parts. If we were going to track down Nemesis—i.e., a supervillain—then we had to think like one. And not only did Serge possess an encyclopedic knowledge of heroes and villains that rivaled my own, but last summer something had happened that suggested to me he would have a deep understanding of the criminal mind.

We had gone to superhero camp together. It's like Boy Scout camp, but with a better theme song. You stay in tents in the woods along with fifty other boys, all of whom know that Galactus, Devourer of Worlds, is only afraid of one thing—the Ultimate Nullifier; that since 1970 the Flash would beat Superman in a race; and that Wolverine was originally going to be called the Badger. In other words, like-minded souls. The brochure says the purpose of the camp is to learn from the good example of superheroes. From my experience its purpose is to run around for a week in the woods wearing a mask and cape and eating junk food until you're sick. When you arrive you're given a superhero name. I was the Indigo Shadow (we were late due to a traffic jam on the highway, and all the good colors had already been taken). Serge was Doctor Cranium.

When the Purple Hood nabbed the last hot dog from under Doctor Cranium's nose at the Friday night barbecue, Serge didn't take it well. In comics you usually discover that a supervillain turned evil because of some terrible event in his past, like the death of a family member or because he was exposed to some ancient cursed object. For Serge his evil trigger was a frank in a bun. I found him later that evening attempting to divert the river to flood the camp, standing atop a pile of logs swearing to the night sky that he would cleanse the world of the dratted Purple Hood.

Serge's villainous streak would serve us well in our quest to track down Nemesis.

Last night I had explained this to Lara.

There was one more good reason I wanted Serge along for the ride. I didn't feel comfortable going on a mission with Lara, just the two of us. I knew that she was highly capable. It was just that . . . I didn't want her thinking we were on a date.

I'd seen boys who'd been on dates with girls. One week they'd be sitting around after class happily discussing whether Batman would beat Iron Man in a fight, or if Aquaman really is useless out of water. The next they'd be putting gunk in their hair, mumbling out of one corner of their mouths, and sharing earbuds with girls in order to listen to awful music. One, that can't be hygienic. And two, when you tried to show them your latest issue of Fantastic Four, they'd act all cool and grumpy and then slouch off to the boys' bathroom to smear on more hair gunk. If that's what dating did to you, then I wanted no part of it.

I had not explained this to Lara.

"So, my friends," said Serge, polishing off the fourth finger of a Kit Kat, "what is the purpose of our rendezvous this morning?"

I knew what I was about to tell him would quite possibly overwhelm his brain. The shock might even cause him to have a reaction, like the time in the school cafeteria when Mark Stanton accidentally ate a kiwi stuffed with peanut butter and his head blew up like a purple balloon. So I had prepared a checklist, which was pinned to my Martian Manhunter clipboard.

I asked the first question. "Are you carrying a full dose of your asthma medication?"

"Yes." Serge presented the loaded inhaler. "Why are you asking me this?"

"In a minute," I said, tapping my pen against the clipboard. "We haven't done the checklist." I cleared my throat. "Have you experienced any palpitations lately?"

"I do not know this word, *pal-pee-tay-shuns*."

Lara tutted impatiently. "He means are you likely to drop dead if you hear something shocking?"

Serge looked from Lara to me. "What is she talking about? What is this shocking thing?"

I lowered the clipboard and said in a solemn voice, "Serge, I have something to tell you."

He clutched his belly. "Oh no, I am sick, aren't I? I knew it." He glanced down. "I told *maman* that the itching was grave."

Lara palmed her face. "You're not sick. How would

Luke know if you were sick? He's not a doctor." She looked at me pleadingly. "For goodness' sake, just tell him."

There were still sixteen questions on the clipboard that we hadn't covered, but I could see from Lara's expression that they would remain unanswered. "Serge, you know my big brother, Zack?"

"Yes."

"You know Star Guy?"

"Of course."

I took a deep breath. "They are one and the same."

DANCE!

Serge gazed at me blankly.

"No wonder he's looking at you like that," said Lara. "I mean, that was an odd way to put it. 'They are one and the same.' Why couldn't you just have said, 'Hey, Serge, my brother is Star Guy'?"

There was a squeak, as if millions of hamsters had cried out in shock and were suddenly silenced. We looked around to find Serge flat on his back on the ground, mumbling in French. Or it might have been Klingon. I get them confused.

Lara knelt beside him. "Do you need your inhaler?"

Serge shook his head and continued to babble. His skin went gray and then red and back again, like a chameleon refereeing a squirrel fight.

"Serge, how many fingers am I holding up?" I asked.

Lara glanced at me, puzzled. "Uh, you're holding them behind your back."

"Yes?"

"So, how's he supposed to see?"

"Fourteen!" yelled Serge, sitting up with a jolt.

"Correct!" I beamed, helping him to his feet. "He's fine," I informed Lara. For some reason she seemed confused.

"Your brother . . . your brother," Serge spluttered. "Your brother, he is"—he gripped my arm, digging his fingers into the muscle and staring at me wide-eyed, as if someone had just stuck a needle in his butt for medical reasons—"Star Guy?" he said, his voice barely above a whisper.

I nodded.

"Granted cosmic superpower . . ." he began.

I rolled my eyes. Not this again.

"In our darkest hour . . ."

Despite his best efforts, but to no one's surprise except Serge's, his oath had not caught on.

"Star Guy, star light,

Protector of the world tonight!"

Hope and delight and astonishment shone from his eyes. It was quite touching really, but didn't take away from the sheer awfulness of the oath.

Morning recess would be over in five minutes, which was just enough time to bring Serge up to speed on everything that had happened.

When I'd finished he asked, "Are you certain that Star Guy said 'volcano'?"

I frowned. "What else could he have said?"

Serge pursed his lips thoughtfully. "Vol-au-vent?"

"What's vol-au-vent?"

"It is a small, hollow puff pastry typically with a savory filling, although sometimes it can be sweet."

"No," I said after a long pause. "I'm pretty sure he said 'volcano.'"

"But it doesn't make sense," said Lara. "If there was a volcano in the middle of the city, we'd know about it."

"You wouldn't if it was hidden," I suggested.

"How do you hide a volcano?" she snapped.

I listed the most obvious ways on my fingers. "Distract-o-Beam, invisibility cloak, maybe it goes up and down on a hinge."

"A *folding* volcano?" She sounded unconvinced.

"Oh, yes. Your typical supervillain has access to loads of impressive camouflage tech. Isn't that right, Serge?"

Serge agreed with a grunt. "You could also suspend it in a cloud of Hypno-gas or disguise it as an innocent apartment building."

With that kind of smart thinking, it was obvious why I wanted Serge along on the mission, but I could see that he was still reeling from shock. Did he fully understand what he was getting into? I had to be sure. This was no comic. We were going up against a maniac supervillain holed up in an invisible volcano . . .

OK, so it was somewhat like a comic.

But this was real life. We might die. And there would be no writer to bring us back again in the next issue with a magical infinity formula.

I had to lay it on the line for Serge.

"The mission will be extremely dangerous," I said. "We might not all make it back."

"*Pah!* Danger, it is my middle name," he said with another of those dismissive waves.

"It is?" asked Lara. "Is that a French name?"

"You misapprehend. It is not actually my middle name; it is something you say to show that you are not scared."

Lara's expression hardened. "One thing's bothering me, and I'm sorry, but I have to say it. How do we know that Nemesis hasn't already"—she looked away awkwardly—"y'know?"

No, I didn't know. "What?"

"Well, if I was Nemesis—which I'm not—and I had captured my arch-foe, Star Guy, I wouldn't hang around. I'd . . . well . . . he's your brother. I don't want to say."

"I thought you said you *had* to say."

"Yes, but it's difficult to say."

Serge nodded grimly. "I shall say." Thankfully, he understood what she was driving at. "She means how do we know that Nemesis hasn't already"—he drew a finger sharply across his neck and made a rasping sound—"*disposed* of Star Guy?"

Lara grabbed my arm. "Oh, Luke, I'm sorry, but it's a possibility we have to face."

I wasn't concerned at all. "Hasn't happened."

She frowned. "But how can you be so sure?"

"Simple. No public gloating."

"Uh, what does that mean?"

It was perfectly obvious. "Supervillains don't just kill heroes, not without first boasting to the world that they're going to do it. They take control of all the TVs and the Internet and broadcast a message from their hideout, smirking about how they're going to bump off the superhero in question so that they can take over the world, and then they say 'Nothing can stop me now.' And then they laugh. Hideously."

I could see Serge nodding in agreement throughout my explanation. "What my friend says is correct. Star Guy lives." He flicked his eyes from Lara to me. "At least for now."

Recess ended, and we headed to the gym for our next

class, which was dance. This term we were making our way through the Greek myths. Today we were dancing the story of the Twelve Labors of Heracles (or Hercules, if you're Roman). Not all Twelve Labors, because that would have been completely exhausting. The dance that morning was about an incident in his childhood, when Heracles first demonstrated his powers. Heracles was half man, half god, and he had a half brother, Iphicles, who was a mere mortal. In the Greek myths all regular people are described as "mere mortals." When they were babies, Heracles showed off his superhuman strength by saving Iphicles from a sneak snake attack. I suppose he was an ancient Greek superhero. I wondered how Iphicles felt about his brother.

Mrs. Tyrannosaur sat at the piano, claw hands poised above the keys, peering at us over her spectacles. "Ready, class? And, one-two-three . . ."

She began to play a sad, swoopy tune called "The Lament of the Wine Dark Sea." Although it was a piece of music about another time and place, it made me feel the loss of Zack deep in my belly. It also made me regret all the terrible things I'd said to him that night. With a pang of guilt I wondered if I'd ever get a chance to apologize. Mrs. Tyrannosaur bent over the keys, producing sad-sweet music from the ancient piano. In answer, thirty pairs of feet thumped against the wooden floor of the gym.

As we waved our arms and shuffled our feet in an effort to tell the story of Heracles, Lara, Serge, and I snatched moments to discuss our mission. Our first objective was to track down Nemesis's hideout. You'd think finding a volcano in the suburbs would be easy, but when we'd put our town's name and "volcano" into Google, the search had come back with the local Volvo dealership. That was the trouble with secret lairs—they weren't very well marked.

"Per'aps there are plans at the Council office?" suggested Serge, arms stretched to the ceiling, pretending to be a pillar. "Remember all that fuss when Ikea desired to open a new superstore. Think of the objections a volcano would cause."

Lara slithered past as one of the snakes. "I don't think supervillains apply for planning permission."

I was a Greek urn, which is called an amphora. To dance the part of earthenware is harder than you'd think. I closed my eyes and pictured the hot flames of the kiln as I twirled and leaped. You probably think I would hate dance class, but you'd be wrong. Yes, I'm a terrible dancer—I take after my mom and dad—but the funny thing is it doesn't seem to matter. Something happens to me when I'm whirling around, narrowly avoiding collisions with my classmates. It's like when I read a really good issue of X-Men and become caught up in the story, and everything else in my life fades into the background. When I'm throwing my body around my mind is clear to think. Mrs. Tyrannosaur calls it an "immersive activity." And at that moment I was immersed in the puzzle of finding Zack.

We did have one lead: our prime suspect in the search for Crystal Comics's security footage.

"We need to find Walter Go," I said, coming out of a pirouette. "If he has the missing video, then I'd bet my comic collection he knows something about Zack's kidnapping."

Serge wheezed, and his eyes went wide. "Your *whole* collection?"

That might have been a bit rash. "Well, obviously not Grant Morrison's JLA run, or Stan Lee and Steve Ditko's The Amazing Spider-Man, or Neil Gaiman's Sa—"

"We get it," said Lara.

We joined hands and all looked to our left, so that we could dance the frieze, which is the sculpted picture above the columns on a temple.

Walter Edmund Go. The name scrolled through my mind like a banner trailing behind a light aircraft.

Something about it had bothered me since the first time I'd heard Christopher Talbot speak the name. It was both strange and strangely familiar.

I was concentrating so hard that I didn't notice the vaulting apparatus until it was too late. I bounced off its high wooden side and landed awkwardly on the floor. I let out a cry. But I didn't care about the pain from my throbbing foot, and as I watched it swell up like an inflatable turnip, a smile spread across my face.

I had solved the mystery of Walter Edmund Go.

23

WALTER EDMUND GO

"*There is no* Walter Edmund Go," I declared excitedly.

"Are you having the meatloaf?" asked Serge. Fair to say, that was not the response I had expected.

The last lesson before lunch had finished, and a line of noisy, ravenous kids filed into the cafeteria. When dance class had ended we'd gone straight into science, so there had been no opportunity for me to tell the others about my brilliant deduction until this moment.

Serge couldn't concentrate on anything less than a full stomach, so I forgave him. We hovered between the salad bar and the meatloaf in question.

"Of course there's a Walter Go," Lara objected, sliding a tuna salad onto her tray.

"Walter *E.* Go," I repeated, emphasizing his middle initial.

There was a crunch as Serge bit into a breadstick. "I do not comprehend. Why are you saying his name like that? What is the significance of Walter E. Go?"

We took our trays and sat down at our usual table.

"Superheroes and villains have one thing in common," I explained. "Most live behind a secret identity. Clark Kent is Superman. Matt Murdock is Daredevil. Princess Diana of Themyscira is a mouthful, and she's also Wonder Woman. There is another phrase for this: alter ego. And what does that sound like?"

Lara gasped. "Walter Ego!" I could see her mind working. It worked fast. "You're saying Walter E. Go is just another name for Christopher Talbot?"

I pierced the straw through my carton of not-from-concentrate apple juice.

"Talbot lied to us," I said, taking a suck. "That day we went to his house asking questions, we were getting too close to the truth. He had to say something to put us off the scent. So he used his alter ego."

"But why does the owner of a comic book store need an alter ego?" puzzled Serge.

"Because he's not just an innocent comic book store owner," I said. "I believe he's behind Zack's kidnapping." I gulped the last of my juice and crushed the carton in my fist for dramatic effect. "I believe that Christopher Talbot is Nemesis."

Serge swallowed a forkful of mashed potato.

"Are you sure?" Lara asked doubtfully. "Let's look at the facts—a good reporter doesn't jump to conclusions. When we interviewed him he came across as, well, kind of useless. He was so . . . *bumbling*. All that business with the jetpack going through his ceiling—surely an experienced supervillain would *never* allow that to happen."

I had an answer for that. "I think his bumbling was a trick to distract us from the truth."

"Pardon," said Serge, raising a hand as if he was in class, "but what is this *bumbling?*"

"It means behaving clumsily," I said. "Lots of superheroes' alter egos are bumblers. Clark Kent is the most famous one. When he trips over things and plays with his glasses it distracts people from the truth."

"I knew it!" said Lara, spearing a cherry tomato with her fork. "I knew he had to be the villain the moment he opened the door."

"But you just said we shouldn't jump to conclusions and that he was a bumbler."

She waved away my objection.

"Never mind that now," she said. "I saw right through his little game. I knew Christopher Talbot was a weirdo. All those freaky gadgets and that odd little robot." She shuddered. "Nobody pulls the whale over my eyes."

I wanted to say that he hadn't pulled the whale—

wool—over my eyes either, but if anyone should be wearing the Wooly Ski Mask of Shame, it was me. The truth was I'd liked him. All the things that Lara found weird, I admired. Above all, he and I shared the same deep love of comic books.

Lara went on.

"So, Christopher Talbot has the missing video of Star Guy." Having finished her tuna she tapped a spoon thoughtfully against her bowl of seasonal fresh fruit salad. "And when you turned up on his doorstep he recognized *you* from the same video. Then he tricked us into giving him your address so he could kidnap Zack. Clever. *Fiendishly* clever."

I felt betrayed by Christopher Talbot and everything I'd thought he stood for. How could a lifetime of reading superhero stories turn someone into a villain? It went against everything I believed.

But then I remembered a conversation I'd had with my dad when we watched Star Wars together. I'm talking about the first films—the original trilogy. They're so old that the first time Dad put them on I expected they'd be in black-and-white. He had been desperate to show them to me since he tucked me into my first Jedi onesie (I'm "Luke" for a reason), but Mom decided I had to wait until I was old enough, which in her opinion was eight. Dad argued for four. They settled on six. We watched the trilogy together on my birthday, beginning our marathon session shortly after dawn. Dad kept me home from school, and he called in sick to work, cupping the phone to explain to me in a whisper that this was a special occasion. And not to tell Mom. We watched all three films back-to-back. Then we watched *Empire* again because it's the best.

When it was over he turned to me with a tear in his eye and asked who my favorite character was. Well, that was obvious: Luke Skywalker, my namesake, the young Jedi with the superpower of the Force. Dad said that when he watched it the first time, Luke was his favorite too. But years later when he revisited the films, he preferred the roguish, gun-slinging Han Solo. I liked Han—not nearly as much as Luke—but I could see how someone might prefer him. But then Dad had lowered his voice and said that when he was older still he found himself drawn neither to Luke nor Han.

"Not to Princess Leia?" I squirmed.

"Well, no. I mean, yes. But no." He hauled himself out of his armchair and walked in front of the TV. Behind him the end credits crawled across the screen. "The character I liked most was—" he paused for what seemed an age—"Darth Vader."

No-o-o-o!

In that instant I pictured the Dark Lord extending his gloved hand to me and in that cold, rumbling voice saying, "Luke, I am your father's favorite."

I was shocked, as if someone had fired a proton torpedo down my thermal exhaust port.

Slowly I began to form a picture of the world I was being raised into. You start off believing in the good guys until one day you find yourself cheering for the Dark Lord of the Sith. Is everyone eventually tempted by the dark side? Is that what had happened to Christopher Talbot? And would it happen to me one day?

Something was moving rapidly inches from my face. "Luke?" My eyes focused on Lara's waving hand.

"Hmm?" I said.

"You zoned out. Where were you?"

"Far, far away."

"Well, get back here because we need to figure out our next move."

As we drew up our plans the cafeteria emptied around us. The familiar uproar of lunch faded to the occasional clink of cutlery. The three of us were among the last to leave.

"So, we're agreed," said Lara finally. "After school we stake out Talbot Grange, and when Christopher Talbot—

aka Nemesis—appears, we follow him. At some point he has to pay a visit to his secret volcano. We just make sure that we're on his tail when he does."

I nodded. It was a solid plan. I knew that there would be obstacles along the way. I was prepared for things like booby traps, robot guards, and searchlight towers. But the first complication appeared sooner than I'd expected—that very afternoon at the school steps.

24

THE BEGINNING OF THE END

"But, Dad . . ."

"Luke, no arguments. We're going home."

"But Serge and Lara—"

He raised a warning finger. "Don't make me use my Jedi mind trick on you."

I groaned in frustration. "I have to tell them. We made plans."

"I'm sure your plans can wait."

Ha! He had no idea, and it wasn't as if I could tell him what we were really up to.

"I suppose," I mumbled, slouching off.

Lara and Serge lingered by the steps.

"Does your papa permit you to come on the stakeout with us?" asked Serge.

I shook my head.

"It's understandable," said Lara. "Your mom and dad have lost one son; they don't want to risk losing you as well." She gave me a comforting smile. "Don't worry, we've got this. Serge and I will find Nemesis's lair."

I was struck by a horrible thought. "You won't mount an assault on the volcano without me, will you?"

"No, Luke. Of course not." She squeezed my arm. "You can lead the assault"—a shadow of doubt fell across her face—"as long as you're allowed out of your room."

When Dad and I got home, Mom gave me a hug like I'd just returned from an expedition to the South Pole. I could hear chatter coming from the kitchen. I went in to find both sets of my grandparents making endless cups of tea and cutting slices of very solid fruitcake that you could easily chip a tooth on.

Grandpa Bernard was sitting at the table watching sports on his iPad, which he does a lot when he visits. And he never wears headphones, so the rest of us are forced to listen to some boring commentator drone on about golf or baseball. When someone makes a hole in one or hits a run the crowd applauds, and it sounds like a bunch of mice clapping from inside a can. Very annoying. Grandma Maureen is always scolding him about it, but he never listens, just smiles happily and asks her to make him another cup of tea. They're my dad's parents, and they live on the other side of the country.

My mom's are called Grandpa Clive and Mushki (she hates being called Grandma because she says it makes her sound ancient, so she invented this secret identity to pretend that she's not). They live two streets away. But right then, they were all camped out at our house.

The family was rallying around in the face of Zack's disappearance, and so were the neighbors. A steady stream of them trooped through the hastily repaired front door, leaving cards and casseroles. I didn't know why, but something about the situation made people want to cook meat slowly in large pots.

Cara Lee and her mom stopped in with a card and yet another casserole—chicken and mushroom, fourth of the day. Mrs. Lee sat with Mom and held her hand, and Cara stood looking sad next to the oven. She had written in the card: "To Zack, I'll never forget the way you saved my phone." And then she'd signed her name and put a kiss. Zack would be pleased—if he survived.

Among the jumble of pots on the kitchen table was a piece of mail for me. It had come that morning. I don't receive a lot of mail, mostly birthday cards and notes from school about my behavior/homework/test results/all of the above. It felt like a birthday card, but my birthday had been weeks ago. I slid a thumb under the flap and pried it open. Inside was an oddly shaped card printed with gold lettering.

It was an invitation to the opening of Crystal Comics's new flagship store. In all the drama of the last few days I'd forgotten about Christopher Talbot's offer to invite Lara and me to the launch.

I was confused. Hadn't it just been a trick to obtain my address so that he could kidnap Zack? Judging from the invitation to the grand opening party next week, it appeared that the launch was real enough. What was Christopher Talbot up to? Why did he want me there? When I thought about it, I realized the answer was obvious. Like all the supervillains I'd ever read about, he wanted an audience for his ultimate despicable deed.

I could only guess what monstrous fate he had in store for my brother. Serge's theory was that Christopher Talbot intended to display the kidnapped Star Guy as the centerpiece of his new comic store, like some twisted ice swan sculpture. The sick feeling in my stomach told me that whatever Nemesis had planned for Star Guy, it was a lot darker than turning him into an ice-based party decoration.

"What happened to my golf?" Grandpa Bernard complained, interrupting my gloomy thoughts. He hit his iPad like it was some sort of old-timey TV set that you could fix by banging it on the side.

The rest of us breathed sighs of relief that the commentator's mosquito whine had finally stopped. A new voice took his place, and even through the tinny speaker you could tell that this one sounded serious.

"We interrupt our regular programming for an important announcement. Please stand by."

There were concerned murmurs from the others in the room. In my mind there was only one answer to Grandpa Bernard's question. It had to be Nemesis. He'd taken over the airwaves to broadcast his message of doom.

We crowded around the iPad. A picture of an empty podium with a microphone filled the screen. Behind it on the wall hung an official-looking seal. Dad flicked on the TV. The same image was on there too. As we watched, a figure in a dark suit made her way slowly to the podium. It wasn't Nemesis.

"It's the president," said Mom.

I could hear the concern in her voice. I looked around at the other adults; all of them were worried.

The president removed her glasses and laid them on the podium. I thought she looked tired.

"This morning at four a.m. eastern standard time," she began solemnly, "ATLAS, the Asteroid Terrestrial-impact Last Alert System, detected an object in our solar system on a collision course with Earth." She paused. "The calculations have been verified by NASA. The asteroid will hit our planet in one week.

"Since this morning I have been in close contact with

other world leaders to monitor the situation. Everything humanly possible is being done to avert a catastrophe, but it is my grave duty as your president to prepare you for the worst. The vast size of the asteroid means that an impact will"—she choked and then gathered herself—"will wipe out civilization as we know it."

There was a collective gasp from everyone in our kitchen.

"How big *is* this thing?" said Dad quietly.

It was as if the president had heard him. "The object is approximately seven hundred miles in diameter."

I felt dizzy.

"That's bigger than the Death Star," I muttered in disbelief.

"In accordance with international conventions, NASA has designated the asteroid as . . . Nemesis."

What?! That didn't make sense. Nemesis was Christopher Talbot. Wasn't he?

"Nemesis is coming." That's what Zorbon the Decider had told Zack. Naturally I'd assumed that he or she was a superpowered criminal. But I'd gotten it all wrong.

Nemesis wasn't a supervillain—it was a giant space rock.

Which meant that Star Guy's destiny was to save the world from a planet-killing asteroid. There was just one problem.

Star Guy was a prisoner.

"The brightest minds on our planet are already at work planning how to avert the threat," the president continued. "However, our technological capabilities are limited in the face of such a galactic scale." She leaned in, gripping the edges of the podium, looking less like a politician and more like someone's mom. "So I make this appeal now to the individual known as Star Guy. This is our darkest hour. Please come forward. Your planet needs you."

The broadcast ended, the screen went dark and was replaced seconds later by golf. No one moved. Then Grandpa Bernard switched off his iPad.

25

AN INVITATION TO ADVENTURE

They canceled school. We had one more day with Mrs. Tyrannosaur, and at the end of the last class she gave out prizes for the best drawing and story, even though the semester wasn't officially over for another two weeks. I knew I'd be leaving elementary school for the last time this year—I just hadn't expected it to be because of a giant asteroid. All year long I'd been anxious about moving up to the big school, but right then my fears about leaving old friends and making new ones, getting lost in unfamiliar hallways and being late for class, not being smart enough and falling behind—all that seemed so tiny and unimportant.

Before we went home, Mrs. Tyrannosaur gave each of us a big hug and told us how much she loved us, and then all our parents picked us up—even the kids who normally walk or take the bus themselves.

Lara, Serge, and I walked out together under a cloud

of hopelessness. The stakeout of Talbot Grange had so far failed to produce the location of the secret volcano, and if we didn't find it by next Tuesday when the asteroid struck, it would be too late. Time wasn't just running out, it was sprinting wildly, waving its arms with its hair on fire.

Mom and Dad were waiting for me outside the school. They were smiling, but I could tell that they were putting on a brave face. I didn't blame them; what was there to smile about? Zack was missing, and it was six days until the end of the world.

"You have to tell them about Zack," whispered Lara. "The world needs Star Guy, and we need help finding him."

The president's appeal for Star Guy's assistance had, of course, resulted in silence from the superhero. Every night the city council would beam his signal into the sky, and every night it would go dark without a response. Online and off, there was furious speculation about why he had failed to answer the call. For some people his silence proved he was a fake. Others were convinced he'd returned to his home planet. A few suggested he'd entered the cocoon form of his evolution and in five days would emerge as Butterfly Man. Only we knew that he was tied up in a volcano and couldn't come to anyone's aid until we had come to his. Which didn't look like happening anytime soon.

Lara was right. If I told Mom and Dad, they'd inform the authorities. A full-scale search with dogs and police and probably Special Forces and helicopters with infrared and thermal cameras would surely uncover Christopher Talbot's volcano lair. So as we took the short walk home through the park from school, I told my parents the story, from the beginning. They listened in silence as we strolled past the swings where Zack and I used to play together and nodded as we wended our way alongside the pond where we'd fed the ducks and played shark attack. By the time Mom was slotting the key in our front door they knew everything.

There was only one problem.

"What d'you mean, they didn't believe you?" asked Lara.

It was later that night, and I was wearing my Human Torch pajamas. I had snuck the family laptop up to my bedroom and was Skyping with her and Serge. I could hear Mom and Dad down below. They weren't dancing badly like they usually did; instead they were arguing and crying. I preferred it when they danced. I couldn't make out much, but I could tell that they were discussing Zack and me.

"They think I've made up the kidnapped superhero story."

"Why would you do that?" asked Serge.

"To protect myself."

"I do not comprehend," he said.

Parents had a weird way of looking at the world. "They think I've invented a superhero fantasy in order to escape from the horrible reality of the situation."

"But the kidnapped superhero story *is* the horrible reality," protested Lara.

I watched the little video image of me in the lower corner of the screen shrug. "I know. But in their minds it's better for me to imagine my brother as Star Guy, rather than picture him dead in a ditch somewhere, or a victim of some awful kidnapper."

"So, they won't tell the police?"

I shook my head. "No chance." I had an idea. "But that doesn't stop *us* from telling them."

I grabbed the house phone, sat back down in front of the laptop, and dialed the local police station.

"Station House. Sergeant Gordon speaking."

"Hello. My name is Luke Parker, and I have vital information regarding the disappearance of Star Guy."

There was a slurping sound like he was drinking coffee, and then the sergeant said, "Is that so?"

He said it as a question, but I got the feeling that he

didn't actually want to know the answer. I filled him in on Zack's kidnapping. When I got to the part about the volcano I could hear him choke.

"So, you'll send out a search party?" I said. "I think six helicopters and twenty-five patrol cars should do it. Oh, and dogs. Yes, lots of tracker dogs. Though you don't need to send the ones with brandy barrels. Unless it snows."

"Thank you for your highly valuable information, sir. In accordance with procedure I shall file it along with the other reports on Star Guy's disappearance. We will action yours in due course."

"OK," I said. Now we were getting somewhere. There was just one thing I wanted to check. "What's 'due course'?"

He cleared his throat. "Based on existing police performance targets and the four hundred or so *other* reports of Star Guy we've had in the last two days, that would be . . . six to eight months."

"What?! But we haven't got that long. Nemesis is coming. Next Tuesday."

"I am well aware of the imminent destruction of the planet, sir." Another sip. "Was there anything else?"

I told him there wasn't and hung up the phone in frustration. "See, this is why in movies the hero never calls the police." Serge and Lara had heard every word of my useless conversation. Their scared faces stared at me from the laptop screen. They were looking at me to do something. Even Lara, who was normally fearless and reckless, seemed to be at a loss. If we failed, it was the end. Of everything.

"So, what are we to do now?" asked Serge.

"We have to find Zack ourselves—no one else is going to help," I said. "It's up to us."

It really was on our shoulders. The governments of Earth had put their best people in a room to come up with a solution to the Nemesis threat, but, according to the twenty-four-hour rolling news coverage, so far all that had come out of the room were requests for pizza.

My eye fell on the invitation to the launch of Crystal Comics's new flagship store, which I'd propped up on the windowsill. The party was scheduled for next Monday, one day before Nemesis was due to impact. I couldn't imagine it would still go ahead, but that wasn't what bothered me. It was something about the odd-shaped invitation. I held it up for a better look. If I'd had Spider-Sense it would be tingling. And then I saw it. My hand started to shake. I turned to Lara and Serge, barely able to speak.

"What have you got there?" asked Lara.

"The invitation . . . from Christopher Talbot."

"Oh, I got one of those too . . ." I could see her rummaging around her desk. "It's kind of strange, having a launch party so close to the end of the world, don't you think?"

"These things, they are planned months ahead," explained Serge. "If he were to cancel now, he would probably lose his deposit on the chair rental."

"Never mind that," I interrupted. "Look at the shape of the card!" I pressed it to my laptop's camera so that it filled their screens.

"It's a triangle," said Serge, mystified.

"It's more like a trapezoid," said Lara.

"No," I said, my voice trembling with excitement. "It's a volcano."

NICE VOLCANO

Early the next morning—as soon as I was able to give my parents the slip—I joined Lara and Serge, and we made our way to the address at the bottom of the invitation. Before long we found ourselves outside the most fabulous comic book store in the soon-to-be-obliterated world. Between an Olive Garden and a Radio Shack rose a volcano on seven floors—Crystal Comics's flagship store.

"It is *be-yoo-tiful*," breathed Serge.

Despite the fact that my brother was almost certainly being held in there against his will, I had to agree. Sloping flanks were scored with what looked like claw marks, but were in fact fissure vents. I knew this thanks to my basic knowledge of vulcanology, which is the study of volcanoes and not Star Trek characters, as I'd originally believed when I borrowed the book from the library. As I watched the fissures ooze with glowing lava, there was a rumble from deep inside the volcano like a dragon clearing its throat, and then a cloud of ash and fire spewed from the crater. The ash cloud and lava were both fake, of course, but the effect was highly impressive. A banner was draped across the front, declaring the grand opening. Incredibly, the party was still on.

"How come we didn't notice this was here before?" Lara asked. "What kind of hi-tech camouflage did Christopher Talbot use? Hypno-gas? Distract-o-Beam?"

"Uhh . . . a tarp," I said, my cheeks coloring. "A *big* tarp," I added, but that didn't make it any better.

We had found Zack's prison; the next thing was to spring him from captivity. That wasn't going to be easy. The volcano was ringed by a high fence topped with razor wire. There was one gate in and out, secured by the kind of weighty padlock that Wolverine would put on the cookie jar to prevent Juggernaut from stealing his snickerdoodles. Multiple surveillance cameras on long poles swayed like king cobras. No patch of ground went unmonitored. As we watched, a crow fluttered over the fence and touched down on the highest wire. There was a crackle of electricity, a bright blue flash, and then a strangled squawk. Its rigid body fell to the ground with a thud.

We went back to my house and assembled in my bedroom to draw up our plan.

"We have a lot of work to do," I said. "One does not simply walk into a heavily fortified secret volcano headquarters."

Faced with the prospect of hard work, Serge opened a packet of salt-and-vinegar chips while Lara used her cub reporter skills to do some quick digging online. On the city council's website she found a downloadable layout of the Crystal Comics building (it turned out that super-villains *did* seek planning permission), and we spent the next few hours devising a brilliant plan.

It didn't start off brilliant. In fact, I'm not sure we ever quite made it beyond "pretty good if overly com-plicated." I wanted to storm the volcano. Serge favored a stealthy approach. We settled on "infiltration," which I had to convince Lara was not a kind of water purifi-cation system. We pored over the layout until we had come up with a series of inventive methods to gain entry, and then Serge pointed out that we had invitations, so if we waited until the launch party we could simply stroll through the front door. That seemed a whole lot easier than my best plan, which involved a zip line, wigs, and a small amount of high explosives.

Lara raised an objection. "There is one bad part to Serge's plan."

"Which is . . . ?"

"The launch party isn't until Monday, the day before

Nemesis is due to hit Earth. That's cutting it close. If we fail, there won't be time for another turn."

Another turn? She made it sound like we were waiting in line for a roller coaster.

"We won't fail," I said firmly. "We can't."

We printed out the layout, unrolled it on my bedroom floor, and gathered around to finalize our tactics. There was some debate about the use of a flamethrower (I was "for" but got outvoted). By the time Mom called us down for lunch, "Operation Star Guy" was good to go.

Our path was filled with peril, and the threat of failure dogged every step, but there was something irresistibly exciting about the promise of adventure. Was this how Zack felt each time he stepped out as Star Guy? My whole body fizzed, even more than the time Dad let me have a sip of sparkling wine. I felt as if I could fly faster than a speeding bullet and leap tall buildings in a single bound. Looking into the faces of my friends, I knew with the force of a Hulk uppercut that we had it in us to pull this off.

I know what you're thinking. I'm getting carried away. I'm in danger of saying something about the power of friendship being more powerful than a supervillain and his army of evil minions. Well, no, that would be silly. Frankly, at that moment I would happily have traded Serge for a well-stocked utility belt.

After lunch, Lara doodled in the margin of the building layout.

"Let's say we do rescue Zack in the nick of time," she said. "Do you really think he can save the world? After all, the reason Christopher Talbot was able to kidnap him in the first place is because he's lost his powers."

I hadn't thought of that. Didn't superheroes always save the world? But Lara was right: without his powers Star Guy was just an ordinary boy.

"Zorbon put his trust in Zack," I said.

But I wished that Zorbon had been a bit less mysterious about his powers. I know you don't get a handbook in situations like these, but a troubleshooting guide would've been useful. I doubted we could reset Zack's superpowers by turning him off and then on again. So why had he lost them in the first place? And how were we going to restore them?

There was a crunch from the other side of the room. Serge's unfinished bag of chips had dropped from his hand and he had accidentally stepped on them. He stood at the window, his back set rigidly toward us, his attention gripped by something outside.

"I think you two had better see this," he said nervously.

Strong winds had driven away the leaden clouds that had squatted over the country for days. The gusting wind was like a bad-tempered teenager, kicking up stones from the street to hurl them at windows, pushing over old ladies, and grumbling all day and night. On TV the weather report called it "atmospheric conditions" caused by the approaching asteroid. The short-term forecast was gloomy. There was no long-term forecast.

"There." Serge pointed to the horizon. Above the slate roofs and chimneys the blue sky hung like a freshly laundered cape. But in one corner was a small black spot edged in fire. No stain remover in the universe would have any effect on this spot. It blazed through the darkness of space on an unstoppable collision course. And in the wind's endless howl, I could hear the words, over and over.

Nemesis is coming.

27

NINE THOUSAND ONE HUNDRED AND TEN

It was the day before the end of the world.

As it drew ever closer Nemesis loomed larger, an immense thumb reaching down from the heavens to squash a bug—and we were the bug. Fragments broke off the main body of the rapidly approaching asteroid, and already the first impacts were happening around the world. The skies were streaked with fire as chunks of burning rock punched through our atmosphere. Tracking stations across the globe monitored their unerring course, and alarming news reports came in every few hours. Most of the fragments landed harmlessly in the oceans, but a few struck cities. New York, Paris, Beijing, all of them suffered. We were not immune. The Glades Mall took a direct hit. All that remained was the Filene's and a bit of Auntie Anne's Pretzels. No one was killed, but it was bad for me, since I had a twenty-dollar gift card to Ben & Jerry's that I hadn't yet spent.

In their secure room in a top-secret location, the brightest and best minds on the planet had been eating pizza and hatching plans. Over the course of the last week they had emerged to suggest various strategies to avoid the total destruction of the planet. Most of them sounded like plots to expensive Hollywood blockbusters. Converting the earth's core into a giant engine and driving it out of the asteroid's path? Check. Blasting the moon into the asteroid to knock it off course, like a cosmic pool shot? Check. But the plan that the world's leaders settled upon was even worse.

You know how there's always that scene at the end of the film when the good guys finally get their starship back and the bad guys' shields are down, and the captain shouts "Fire everything!" Well, that was their plan. Every country on the planet was going to aim its entire arsenal of nuclear weapons at the asteroid and fire at the same time. It was crazy. It was dangerous. It was doomed to failure.

I made a quick calculation (on the back of a pizza box, funnily enough). I reckoned that even if seventy-five percent of the missiles hit the target—which would be remarkably accurate—it would be like firing a peashooter at a charging elephant. And if the asteroid didn't finish us off, the radiation from the missiles that exploded in the atmosphere would make the surface of the earth uninhabitable for fifty thousand years. The aftermath would be like one of those other movies—the kind in which there's a handful of human survivors who have to eat cold beans forever and live underground, and everyone else has three noses and zombies around in a barren radioactive wasteland. Perhaps the only thing worse than the plan itself was what they'd decided to name it: Operation Spitting Umbrella. I mean, you could see what they were getting at, but come on. Surely they could have come up with something snappier.

The smartest people on the planet weren't the only ones who'd gone nuts. With the clock counting down to the end of their lives, most people on Earth were acting crazy and, in a lot of cases, behaving badly. For instance, all the people without big TVs started stealing them from all the people *with* big TVs, but then the first group must have realized that they didn't want to waste the little time they had left watching TV, so that was the end of all the stealing. There was a great deal of crying, which was understandable. Then there was the kissing. You couldn't ride your bike down any street without running over a dozen couples canoodling. Didn't they know that during the average kiss, five million germs are swapped between the participants? I could only suppose that with the extinction of the human race approaching they didn't really care about the effect of a few hundred bacteria colonies.

The night before, Lara and I had sat in the doorway of the tree house, our legs dangling down into the quiet darkness of the yard, our eyes fixed up at the noisy sky. (*Not* kissing.)

"How many stars do you see?" I asked her.

She frowned in concentration, and for a moment I thought she was making a serious attempt to count them. After a few seconds she blew out in exasperation, "Millions."

"Uh-uh." I shook my head. "If you live somewhere really dark, then according to the Bright Star Catalog you can see nine thousand one hundred and ten stars with your naked eye." Lara looked at me in amazement. "I know! You'd think it'd be millions, but it's not."

She tilted her face up to the now-slightly-less-infinite sky, paused, and said, "Nine thousand one hundred and *eleven*."

I knew what she meant. Technically, Nemesis wasn't a star, so wouldn't make it into the Bright Star Catalog, but I wasn't going to argue. It was so close now that it hung almost level with the moon, two great silver circles like the unblinking eyes of a wolf from a fairy tale. A giant, devouring space wolf. With two major light sources the nights weren't as dark as usual. The whole world had never been brighter, which was backward, since it was about to be extinguished. The extra light cast strange night shadows and made it hard to sleep. When I did I had strange dreams.

In one of them I was sitting in the tree house with Lara. Nemesis was heading straight for us. There was a great rushing wind, and the asteroid struck the tree. But the old oak didn't break. It creaked and groaned and bent all the way to the ground, but we hung on, and then it whipped upright and, like a rock from a catapult, sent the asteroid flying back into space. I know that dreams are supposed to mean something important, but I think that one was just wishful thinking. And I don't know why Lara was in the dream, but when I woke up I was glad that she was.

Mom, Dad, and I sat down to breakfast for what everyone assumed would be the last time. Mom put out Zack's Cheerios, as she had done every day since he'd gone missing, and glanced at his empty chair. Dad laid a hand on top of hers and squeezed it gently. She sniffed, gave a tiny shake of her head, and said in a cheery voice,

"What would you like this morning, Luke? How about pancakes?"

I could tell that she wasn't as cheery as she wanted me to think.

"Yes, please," I said.

A good breakfast was essential on any normal day, but I'd need all the energy I could store up for tonight's mission. "With two eggs, please."

"Two eggs for a growing boy," she said, and then her smile slipped.

It must have occurred to her that, barring a miracle, the height I was today would be as tall as I'd ever grow. Dad would never scratch another mark into the height chart on the kitchen wall. Mom sat down, put her head in her hands, and sobbed quietly. Dad put his arm around her and said comforting words. He looked across the table at me, and I could see that his eyes were damp. And not the kind of damp they'd been after we'd watched Star Wars together for the first time.

Ever since Zack had gone missing Mom and Dad had endlessly circled the neighborhood sticking posters to every lamppost, wall, and tree trunk. But now even the police had given up looking for him. I slipped off my chair and walked around the table. Stretching my arms as wide as they would go, I hugged them both. I wanted to tell them that they shouldn't worry, that everything would turn out all right, but I couldn't.

The whole family had decided to spend the last full day on planet Earth together. Lara and Serge were with their families too. We'd agreed to rendezvous after dark. The question was how we would get through this most unusual day. Mom had decided to cook a big feast, Grandpa Bernard had brought his crossword book (since all the golf had been canceled), *Home Alone* was showing on three different channels, and the president was due to address the nation. It was a lot like Thanksgiving, except instead of turkey we were having a giant asteroid.

"At least it's a nice day for it," said Grandpa Bernard, as if he was talking about a trip to the beach and not the last day of the human race.

He was right—a bit bonkers, but right all the same. Until this week the country had been covered in a thick band of clouds that stretched from coast to coast. It was like living under the dreariest blanket knitted by the most miserable grandma in the whole world. At night you couldn't see a single star in the sky.

The clouds. Something about the clouds . . .

It hit me like a punch from Colossus.

It had been cloudy the week Zack was kidnapped. In

that instant I knew why his force field had died, why his telekinesis had given up the ghost, why he couldn't breathe underwater.

"Zack needs starlight to recharge his powers!" I muttered under my breath.

The final missing part of our plan was in place: all we had to do was expose Zack to the stars, and he'd recharge like a plugged-in iPhone.

The day drew on slowly, and then all of a sudden it was over, like curtains coming down at the end of the school play.

Mom and Dad insisted on tucking me into bed, even though I am far too old for such shenanigans. I wasn't tired, of course, but pretended to be in order to carry out my mission. It's called a *ruse*.

Mom adjusted my pillow. "Are you sure you don't want to stay up longer?"

The world really was ending if my parents were asking me to stay up past my bedtime.

"Just another ten minutes?" said Dad.

I faked a yawn. "But I'm so tired."

They sat on the edge of my bed, and I could see them exchange awkward glances, as if deciding who should go first, and then Mom said, "Luke, we need to have a talk."

Dad chimed in. "If Operation Spitting Umbrella doesn't work . . ."

"It won't," I said firmly.

"It might," said Mom, but I could tell that she didn't believe it herself. I don't think anyone in the whole world believed it was going to save us, even the geniuses who'd come up with it in the first place.

"Is there anything you want to know?" asked Mom.

I didn't know what she was getting at. "About what?"

"About what happens next," said Dad.

"Oh, that's easy," I said. "According to the latest projections, the impact will smash the earth into three giant pieces. But without the mass of the whole planet, there will be no gravity, and the atmosphere will rush out as if someone left the door open in a hurricane. The entire population of the world will be dead within eight minutes."

I could see from their faces that this wasn't the conversation they'd been planning. "Oh, you meant heaven and stuff."

"Well," Mom began, "yes."

I liked the idea of heaven. I mean, it's a secret headquarters full of glowing people with wings. But was it real? Would we all meet up again there when we died? Would I get wings? I could tell that my parents were reaching for something to say that would give me comfort in the face of tomorrow's extinction, but talk about heaven just created more questions. Dad tried another approach.

"You know that the carbon and oxygen that made all life on Earth came from dying stars," he said. "So, in a way we're all Star Guys."

"But we don't all have superpowers," I said.

"I think you do," he said.

My Captain America duvet slipped off as I sat up with a start. Could it be true? Was my dad about to reveal the secret I had suspected my whole life? That I wasn't just a boring, everyday boy from the suburbs? That the tiny spacecraft that carried me from my alien home world crash-landed in the backyard of an ordinary family, and I am actually a prince from another galaxy with a destiny and incredible powers? I knew it!

"I mean, obviously you don't have the sort of superpowers that let you fly or fight crime," said Dad.

Oh.

"What your dad's trying to say," said Mom, "is that we all have powers."

Dad stroked my forehead. "And it's such a damn shame you won't get a chance to grow into yours."

Once I'd confirmed that they weren't saying we were a family of superheroes, and that the powers in question were things like "creativity" and "humor" and "passion," and not "flying" and "teleportation" and "adamantium claws," we said good night.

Mom kissed and hugged me until I thought my head was going to pop off like a cork from a bottle.

Then Dad leaned down and kissed me too and whispered really quietly, "May the Force be with you. Always."

The door clicked softly behind them. I waited until I could hear them downstairs talking with the others, and then I threw off the blankets and hastily pulled on my clothes. My luckiest underpants were in the laundry, which was bad planning, so I settled on my second-luckiest pair. Two minutes later I crept downstairs and slipped out of the back door. I collected the equipment I needed for the mission—concealing it in my Deadpool backpack—and set off to join my friends, who were waiting at the end of the road.

I felt bad sneaking out on my parents, so I don't want you to think I was completely thoughtless. I left a note, telling them where I'd gone, just in case I didn't make it back. And I put in some mushy stuff about how much I loved them and how they were the best parents in the galaxy, even if Dad had questionable taste in movie heroes.

28

SUPERVILLAINS UNLIMITED

The night was filled with the wail of sirens, the squeal of stolen car tires, and the beat of wild music. The streets heaved with hundreds of people dancing crazily by the light of hastily set bonfires. Across the city dozens of fires like a string of beacons lit up the sky. The smoky stench of burning buildings was carried on the air. It was the last night on Earth, and our town had decided to go out with a bang.

As we stood across the road from the comic store, a procession of cars pulled up out front and deposited their passengers. From the first car stepped Lex Luthor and Magneto. They were followed closely by Doctor Doom and Brainiac. The next car after that held Mystique and Doc Octopus. They joined a long line that snaked to a small door in the base of the volcano.

Everyone at the launch of the new Crystal Comics was a supervillain.

Not that this came as any great surprise. I fished out my invitation. Next to where it said RSVP was the instruction: dress evil. As we joined the line we passed General Zod, another Lex Luthor, and six Catwomen climbing out of a minibus.

"That's not fair," complained Lara, watching the posse slink past.

She, too, had dressed as Catwoman, despite my repeated warnings.

"But may I say," said Serge, "that you are *la* most enchanting Catwoman I have seen tonight."

Serge was smooth. He didn't have an invitation of his own, but each of ours included a "plus one," which meant we could bring someone. I think Christopher Talbot had put it there so we could bring along a responsible adult. But by that point I didn't think there was a single responsible adult left on the planet. Instead I had brought Serge, who was dressed as Loki, the Norse God of Mischief.

"Thanks, Serge," said Lara. "Catwoman has a whip, but I have this jump rope, which is a really good substitute, don't you think?"

She held up the tattered old rope for his inspection. He made encouraging noises and nodded enthusiastically, but I knew what he was thinking: her costume was terrible. However, even I wasn't dumb enough to say that to her face. She was wearing a black leotard, black jeans, and rain boots. On her face she'd drawn a pair of whiskers using her big sister's eyeliner pencil. The only cool part of her costume was the mask, which I'd lent her.

"You look good too," she said, admiring Serge's outfit. "You make a great Lucky."

"Loki," he corrected her, adjusting his preposterously horned helmet, tightening the belt on his customized bathrobe, and gripping his broom-handle Chitauri scepter.

"OK, everyone has their mission assignment," I said. "You know what to do once we're inside?"

They nodded. I drew out Zack's phone. Lara had "borrowed" her sister's, which on any other night would have been the most terrifyingly dangerous thing she could do. Tonight it wasn't even in the top ten.

"Let's synchronize phones," I said, opening the settings menu.

Serge raised a hand. "Ah, I do not have the phone."

I sighed. "You were supposed to borrow one."

"Here," said Lara, pulling a pink sparkly phone from her pocket and offering it to him.

Serge inspected it with deep suspicion.

"It is a My Little Pony cell phone," he said.

"Actually, it's called a My Little Phoney," she said.

"It is a *fake* My Little Pony phone?"

"No. Not phony, phone-y. Like . . . y'know what? Doesn't matter."

We'd reached the head of the line. A guard on the door, wearing a silver jumpsuit and a futuristic helmet with a red plexiglass faceplate, checked invitations against a guest list. He found our names. Lara and Serge strolled past, but when I walked up, he stuck out a hand.

"You can't come in without an evil costume," he said, his faceplate fogging up with each word he spoke. "So who are you supposed to be?"

I was wearing a green-and-black-striped T-shirt, a pair of cargo pants, and a backpack. "Sandman," I growled.

He raised an eyebrow. "Well, *Sandman*, I have to inspect your backpack."

Grumbling, I slipped it off and handed it over. Loosening the straps, he lifted the top cover and inspected the contents. "Sand?" A series of puzzled puffs appeared on the inside of his plexiglass as he considered whether or not to let me in. A bag of sand, while unusual, did not feature on his list of banned items. With a mumble he waved me past.

I hurried after the others.

"Good thing he didn't look *under* the sand," I whispered, slinging the backpack over my shoulders.

I looked around. We were in. The first part of "Operation Star Guy" had gone off without a hitch. Now came the hard part.

29

TWO HOURS AND COUNTING

We gazed wide-eyed at the impressive sight before us. The center of the volcano was hollow, with a ramp that ran around the edge, corkscrewing up into the distant crater. The walls were painted a color not so much burnt orange as orange that had been dunked screaming into a vat of boiling oil. The volcano-that-was-also-a-comic-book-store was divided into seven levels, with doors leading off the ramp to each floor where customers could buy comics and merchandise. The ground floor had been converted into a dance floor for the launch party. Jutting from the back wall was a stage upon which a DJ dressed as Doctor Doom mixed tunes, his hooded head bobbing, green cape rippling. Music blasted from gigantic circular speakers with glass-clear stands that made them appear to hover in the air. DJ Doom worked a digital controller to play tricked-up dance versions of superhero movie and TV themes.

A Tal-bot carrying a plate of snacks glided up.

"Vol-au-vent?" it inquired.

Serge helped himself to a handful. I took one filled with gray ooze that smelled of damp sneakers but tasted surprisingly pleasant.

The Tal-bot swung around and was about to zip away when I stopped it, asking, "Can I have the plate, please?"

"Greedy-human-boy," it muttered, but handed over the plate as I'd requested. I tipped the remaining vols-au-vent into the nearest trash can and slipped the plate into my backpack. We made our way around the room collecting more serving plates and several trays.

"Come on, let's blend." Lara pulled me onto the dance floor, and Serge tripped after us. Giant skull lamps dangled like cannibal trophies, and the place heaved with partying villains. I searched the grooving crowd for Christopher Talbot, but with so many masks, scars, hoods, and helmets, it was impossible to tell who he was, or even if he was here.

"I do not see him," said Serge.

"He must have more evil things to do," I said, but exactly what those might be was a puzzle worthy of the Riddler himself.

Why *had* Christopher Talbot kidnapped Star Guy?

Under normal everyday circumstances a supervillain would kidnap his superhero foe to prevent him from foiling his evil plan, which could be poisoning the city's water supply or stealing all the gold in the world—that kind of thing. But whatever despicable plan Christopher Talbot had in mind, he had left it a bit late. Cosmic events had overtaken mere supervillainy. The end of the world was tomorrow, so whatever he had up his shiny silver sleeve, did it really matter now? What's the point of taking over the world if the world isn't going to be there once you take it? Even if it was a really cool bit of evildoing—and even if he'd been planning it for years— couldn't he put it off until Star Guy had prevented Nemesis from turning Earth into the biggest pancake in the universe?

"Do you hear that?" asked Lara.

"I don't hear anything," I said, straining to listen.

"Exactly. The music, it's stopped."

There was a sudden chirping of cell phones. All of the guests had received a text message. I read mine with a sense of rising dread. "Oh, no."

"What's wrong?"

Before I could say, there was a blast of trumpets as if Superman was about to go up, up, and away. The walls shimmered, and a picture formed on them. In place of volcanic rock appeared Christopher Talbot—or I should say *Talbots*, plural. He surrounded us on seven floors, his bolt-blue eyes like blocks of purest Arctic ice.

All the Christopher Talbots began talking at once. "Good evening, ladies and gentlemen," he purred. His smile was a thread. "I apologize for my absence at the party, but as most of you will already know there has been a development."

"What's he talking about?" asked Lara.

"It's Operation Spitting Umbrella," I said, showing her the text message.

"News just in from Earth's most brilliant rocket scientists," said Christopher Talbot, his voice dripping with sarcasm. "Nemesis will shortly be in range of our nuclear missiles. In two hours some ten thousand warheads will launch from silos across the planet on an intercept course with our friendly neighborhood asteroid."

From those who hadn't already heard the news via their phones, there came anxious muttering mixed in with a smattering of cheers from the few who still believed the all-out atomic barrage would save us. If—or rather when—it failed, nothing stood in Nemesis's path. Two hours? Life on Earth had less time to run than a Transformers movie.

"There is no cause for alarm." Christopher Talbot angled his head thoughtfully. "Well, obviously, apart from the popgun defense shield meant to deflect the humongous asteroid bearing down on us at twenty-seven thousand miles an hour. *That's* pretty alarming." He laughed, but no one else did. "Oh, come on, really? If you can't laugh in the face of extinction . . . Where are you going? Come back."

Several supervillain guests were making for the exit. Christopher Talbot called after them. "What if I told you that this isn't the end?" The departing guests paused. Alarm turned to intrigue. "Looking around my volcano I see the villains of my childhood: the evil geniuses, the mind controllers, the assassins." His giant heads swung to take in the other side of the room. "The self-replicators, the body manipulators." He smiled as if he was flicking through a family photo album, then placed a hand over his heart. "I am touched by your presence. So much villainy under one roof—who better to witness the greatest act of *superheroism* the world has ever . . ." He stumbled. "Um . . . witnessed."

All of the Christopher Talbots looked up toward the crater. "Fasten your capes, straighten your hoods, hitch up your underpants . . . and I promise you before this night is out, you will be *wowed*."

"What's he talking about?" whispered Lara.

"I don't know," I said, "but I have a very bad feeling."

The screens flickered, and his image faded to be replaced by a digital countdown clock. It displayed one hour and fifty-nine minutes—the exact time left until Nemesis came in range of Earth's nuclear missiles. When we had made our plans, we hadn't figured on Operation Spitting Umbrella complicating the mission. If a fraction of those missiles exploded in the atmosphere—which they undoubtedly would—then all our efforts would be in vain. Harmful radiation would be released, bathing the planet in deadly rays. Even more radiation than created the Hulk, Daredevil, the Fantastic Four, Dr. Manhattan, Phoenix, Captain Atom, and Spider-Man combined. I reset the timer on Zack's borrowed phone and slipped it back into my pocket.

The countdown had begun.

30

SUPERMAN VS. BATMAN

DJ *Doom dropped* a beat; a thumping track shook the speakers and drowned out the anxious discussions circulating the room. A few guests left the party, but most stayed put. Slowly at first, but then with increasing enthusiasm, the supervillains returned to the dance floor. I could see in their faces—or at least in the faces not obscured by masks—what they were thinking. What better way to go out than at the party to end all parties? And what of Christopher Talbot's mysterious promise—was there really hope?

"Over there, the elevator," said Lara with a guarded nod to the back wall.

Next to the DJ's podium, set into the rock, gleamed a pair of silver doors. According to the plans from the city council website, the stairs went up to the sixth floor, which meant the elevator was the only way to access the crater level on the seventh—where Zack had said he was being held.

Lara struck out through the crowd. Serge and I held back for a moment to watch her thread her way past a bunch of boogying Banes. "She is quite the woman, huh?"

"She's eleven," I said sharply. "She likes My Little Pony and doesn't know the one thing in the universe that Galactus is afraid of."

I felt Serge's eyes on me. "You *like* her," he said.

"Sure, I like her." I shrugged.

A knowing expression crossed Serge's face.

"Not like that," I added quickly.

"I think I understand *very* well," said Serge, a small smile playing across his lips.

"No, you do not," I objected.

"Oh, I think I do."

"Do not."

"Do so."

Thankfully, there wasn't time to argue. As we headed after Lara I experienced a sudden and terrible vision of things to come. I turned to Serge, grabbed him by his high Asgardian collar, and pulled him toward me. "If we live through this, and sometime in the future you see me about to put gunk in my hair, slap the bottle out of my hands. Just slap it right out. Will you do that for me?"

He nodded furiously, causing his giant horned helmet to slip down over his eyes. "If it will make you happy."

I relaxed my grip, and he brushed himself off, set his helmet straight, and took hold of his scepter. Lara had already summoned the elevator. It arrived, and we scurried inside. There was an immediate problem.

"There are only six buttons," said Lara, running her hand up the glossy control panel. "Looks like we need a key to access the crater."

She indicated a keyhole set into the topmost part of the panel.

I scanned the crowd. "So who has a key?"

"Christopher Talbot, obviously," replied Lara. "But it's not as if we can ask him to lend it to us."

Lara pulled up the layout of the building on her phone, studied it for a few seconds, then tapped a finger against the screen. "Here. There's some kind of security office on the third floor. I bet they have a key."

I pressed the button. The doors slid shut, and with a jolt the elevator began to ascend.

The crazy party continued on the third floor. Music rose up from below, and every step we took was hindered by a bopping supervillain with a drink and a flapping cape. The hallway was open to the center of the volcano, and only a slim metal rail prevented swaying partygoers from accidentally walking off the edge. We circled around a Kingpin and an Ozymandias and branched off down a short hallway.

When we reached the corner, I stopped and held up a hand. The other two bunched up against me. I made the internationally accepted hand signal for "Remain Quiet. Our Mission Objective Is Just Around This Corner."

"What?" said Lara.

I huffed in exasperation. "What I said was the security office is just around this corner."

"Yes, I know that," said Lara, holding up her sister's phone. "I have a map."

We edged forward for a better look around the corner. The office lay on the other side of the hallway behind a large window. A solitary guard sat with his elbows propped on a desk, helmeted head in his hands, intently studying something I couldn't make out from where we stood. Behind him on the wall was a key holder in the shape of the TARDIS. It was very cool, and I immediately wanted one for my bedroom.

"The elevator key must be up there," I said. "We need to distract the guard. What's he doing?"

"I think he's reading a comic," said Lara, squinting.

"Then I have an idea. There is one thing a true comic book fan cannot ignore," I said darkly.

"No," hissed Serge from behind the corner of the hallway, realizing what I was about to unleash. "You cannot. Must not."

"We have no other option. I'm sorry." I steered Lara into the hallway, in full view of the security guard. "Remember our bus journey to Christopher Talbot's house? When I taught you about superheroes?"

"Yes, I remember."

"You're going to have to use *all* your training."

"But we only got up to 'C.'"

I prayed that it would be enough. "I have a question for you," I said.

Lara braced herself. "Who would win," I asked slowly and loudly, "in a fight between Batman and Superman?"

I searched her face, willing her to come up with a convincing answer. It was possible that at that moment the fate of two worlds hung on Lara's knowledge of superheroes.

"Well," she began hesitantly, "Batman has martial arts training and . . . and gadgets and stuff." Her answer gathered pace as she grew in confidence. "But Superman has super strength and heat vision and can fly. So, it's obvious. The answer is Superman."

"Wrong!" the comic-reading security guard bellowed.

As I'd suspected, at the first sniff of the question he had leaped from his seat and stormed into the hallway.

I sent a furtive nod in Serge's direction. He slipped past the guard and stealthily made his way toward the empty office.

As the guard bellied along the passage, he launched into his answer to the eternal question, punctuating it with prods of his finger, backing Lara and me against the wall as he talked without taking a breath. "As Frank Miller demonstrated in his seminal work, 'The Dark Knight Returns,' the four-issue miniseries released in 1986, when the US government sends Superman to"— he formed air quotes with his fingers—"'remove the Batman,' it is ultimately the Batman who emerges victorious from their epic encounter in Crime Alley. Even if he had to fake a heart attack and get Green Arrow, aka Oliver Queen, to shoot the Man of Steel with a Kryptonite-tipped arrow." Sweat poured off his forehead, and his chest rose and fell like a bullfrog's.

We smiled up at him politely.

Serge strolled past with a wink and quickly opened and closed his hand, flashing the key.

Two minutes later we were back at the elevator.

I glanced at the digital countdown displayed on the inside of the volcano walls. It had taken us almost fifteen minutes to find the key, and we were running out of time. I turned to Serge. When we'd planned the mission, each of us had taken on a role that suited our particular abilities. I was in charge of planning and tactics. Lara was responsible for investigation and leadership under pressure. Serge was given a task that suited his expertise.

"The vending machine is on the fourth floor," I said. "You know what to do."

Serge nodded gravely, took a firm grip on my hand and shook it, and then did the same with Lara's before kissing her cheeks, as usual. We were going our separate ways. The next time we'd all be together again the fate of the worlds would be decided.

"Do not forget this," he said, offering me his Chitauri broom-handle scepter. "*Bon chance, mes amis*," he said and, whipping his bathrobe around him, slipped through the door into the stairwell.

Lara stepped inside the elevator, slid the key into the panel, and turned it sharply. "Seventh floor, here we come." Almost instantly we began to move. She frowned. "What's happening?"

"We're going down," I said. "We have to go *up* to the crater. That's where they're holding Zack. Turn the key the other way."

The elevator kept going down. The numbers on the control panel lit up in sequence, and there was a ping as we dropped through each floor. And when we reached the ground floor, the elevator continued to fall.

ORIGIN STORIES

We were spewed out in a rocky chamber deep inside the volcano. Next to the elevator we'd arrived in was a second shaft and another set of doors. Lara stood in front of them. "Maybe *this* elevator goes to the crater," she said, but despite a careful search, we could find no button to gain access. "It must be controlled from somewhere else," she said, slapping the metal doors with frustration.

I felt the cold fingers of a current of air on my neck and turned around. A high archway was cut into the solid rock; twice as tall as a man, it was fit for a giant.

"Maybe in here," I said.

Listening to the low moan of the draft, we made our way beneath the arch. It was hard to judge the size of the dim chamber beyond, but our voices were swallowed by the shadows and returned to us as faint echoes.

"This isn't on the plans," said Lara quietly.

Black walls sprang from the floor, arching to form a curved roof from which clusters of stalactites hung like fangs. The stalactites were edged with faint light radiating from a bank of computer monitors on the opposite side of the room. From there came the soft whir of air-conditioning units and the chirp of spinning hard drives. I slipped the backpack from my shoulders, the plates inside clinking against each other as they settled on the rough flagstone floor, and leaned Serge's scepter up against the wall.

"Over there," whispered Lara, pointing to a figure in the shadows. "I don't think he's seen us."

Something about the size of the figure and how still it stood made me suspicious. I crept over and saw that it was the powered suit Christopher Talbot had worn when he'd kidnapped Zack. Above it on the bare wall were blueprints for a variety of different exosuit designs.

"Lockheed Martin, NASA, Nuytco Research Ltd.," I read.

The plans were a mixture of other companies' designs and Christopher Talbot's own. He must have stolen them. A glance at the specifications told me that these were far more advanced than the suit we'd already encountered. As my eyes adjusted to the gloom, I began to make out other shapes in the darkness. Parked in front of a slab-sided section of wall sat the low-slung minivan that had spirited away my brother. On the other side of the vehicle lay a row of wooden cases with glass tops, the kind you'd find in a museum. There was a desk lamp set above each case. I switched on the nearest, and light spilled onto the contents. Rocks. Dozens of them, each labeled with a date and a location.

"Sahara Desert, 1989," I read from the label attached to a brown and gray rock the size of a fist. My eyes moved to the next one, a lump of smooth metal that might have sheared off the Silver Surfer.

"Antarctica," I read. "Mount Yamamoto, 1969."

"Meteorites," said Lara, and I agreed with a nod. Before I could speculate further on the reason for their presence, there was a "cluck" from the semidarkness. I spun around. Ranged along the opposite wall was a series of glass boxes. They were stacked one on top of the other, all the way to the ceiling, and ran the whole length of the chamber. There had to be hundreds of them, and all were occupied. Spiders, scorpions, beetles, fire-engine-red ants wiggling their antennae—each box was home to a single creature. The cluck had come from further along, where a slightly surprised-looking chicken tapped its beak against the inside of its glass cell. I took a step closer, and Lara held me back with an outthrust arm.

"Be careful." She cast her eyes up to a sign on the wall. I recognized it instantly. Familiar from all those post-apocalyptic video games, it was the three-leafed shape of a radiation hazard symbol.

"What's going on here?" she asked warily. "Are these things—" she hesitated, horrified at the thought—"radioactive?"

"I think this is some kind of laboratory." I had an inkling of an explanation, but it was so fantastic I didn't want to speak it aloud. I crossed to the bank of computers and sat down. Screen savers displaying panels from dozens of different comics shimmered across multiple monitors. There was a touch pad beside a keyboard. I woke the computer with a light press and inspected the home screen that bloomed to life.

"What are you looking for?" asked Lara, standing at my shoulder.

"Elevator controls. I think you're right about that other elevator—it must go to the crater level." I scanned the icons dotted across the screen. "Roof operation, flight systems . . ." I paused. "Flight systems? Why does he need *that*?"

Lara didn't share my curiosity. "What about this one?" She indicated a folder marked "ELEVATION."

That seemed more promising. I clicked open the folder to find hundreds of video files, many dating back several years. The latest was from just a few days ago.

"Maybe there's a video on how to operate the elevator," Lara suggested.

I clicked on one. An image of a figure in a bulky hazardous-material suit appeared on the screen. It was Christopher Talbot. He stared down the lens of the camera. "December 16th, the Elevation experiment begins," he said, turning away to reveal the rows of glass cases. "Test subject number one." He opened the nearest case and reached in. When he withdrew his hand, squatting on his palm was the fat body of a tarantula. "I have irradiated the arachnid with a combination of radioisotopes cesium-137 and cobalt-60." He held up his other arm. There was an open flap in the sleeve of the biohazard suit, which displayed a portion of bare forearm. He placed the spider against his skin. "I will now stimulate the test subject in order to produce a defensive reaction."

"What's he talking about?" asked Lara.

"He wants it to bite him," I said.

"But why would anyone want a bite from an enormous, hairy, poisonous spider?"

It was so clear to me now. And so . . . crazy. Everything I knew about Christopher Talbot, from his love of gadgets to his comic book obsession, led to one bizarre but logical conclusion.

"He believes it will give him superpowers," I said, stunned at what I was witnessing.

There was a sharp cry from the screen. The spider had sunk its fangs into Christopher Talbot's arm. His face shining with excitement, he presented the bite mark to the camera. "Stage one complete. Now I await . . . elevation!"

I stopped the playback and closed the window. We watched a few seconds of the next video to confirm that it was the same. Judging by the number of videos in the folder, it appeared that Christopher Talbot had been dosing himself with radioactive insect bites for years in the hope that one of them would give him superpowers.

Lara shook her head in quiet disbelief. "And the meteorites?"

I nodded. "In comics there's a long tradition of people coming into contact with meteorites and acquiring superpowers."

My thoughts fell into place like the last few pieces of my S.H.I.E.L.D. Helicarrier thousand-piece jigsaw.

I took a deep breath and said, "He's planning to do the same thing with Zack."

"What?" said Lara "Get him to bite him on the arm?"

That seemed a bit unlikely.

"He wants to take Star Guy's powers," I said.

"Can he do that?"

"I don't know," I said. "But Christopher Talbot's spent years trying to turn himself into a superhero. Look around you: a secret cave, a modified car, super-soldier armor, a hi-tech computer system, giant video screens, a digital countdown, alien meteorites, and radio-active spider bites. It's like every comic I've ever read. But that's all it's been: a fantasy. Until Star Guy. Until now, Christopher Talbot's never had a test subject with actual superpowers."

Could he have found a way to take Star Guy's powers? I scrolled to the latest video file on the list, dated from just a few days ago, clicked the file, and the video began to play.

"May 27th, *human* test subject number one, stage two," said Christopher Talbot into the lens. The biohaz-ard suit was gone, and instead he wore a regular suit. He stepped aside smartly to give the camera a view of the subject in question.

My brother, Zack, lay pinned to an operating table, his arms and legs secured by metal cuffs. A cap bris-tling with electrodes was clamped to his head, wires trailing to a machine that I guessed was monitoring his brain activity. He looked fast asleep, but then his eyelids flickered and he let out a moan. He was in pain. Fear gripped me, and then I felt a surge of anger. How dare Christopher Talbot do this to my brother!

Zack's chest was bared, and it moved up and down to a ragged rhythm. His star tattoos, which had been cold and dark the last time I saw him, now gave off a weak, irregular glow. Christopher Talbot stood over him. I didn't recognize their surroundings as the chamber we were currently in; it had to be the crater room.

"I have exposed the subject to ten seconds of starlight and, as predicted, the luminosity has partially replenished his superpowers." He gave a thin smile. "Though he remains too weak to break his titanium bonds. I shall now increase the level of starlight." He moved to a touch screen and selected a control interface from a menu. From above came the hum of machinery and a low, grinding noise. At the top edge of the screen, I could make out the crater roof sliding open to reveal the night sky. With the clouds gone, starlight flooded the crater and Zack's weakened body. His star tattoo began to glow as his superpowers recharged.

"Initiating superpower acquisition process," said Talbot, placing a second cap on his own head and carefully positioning electrodes all around his cranium.

He flipped a series of switches on the control panel, and a flying saucer–shaped device descended from the ceiling to hover inches above Zack. I glimpsed a set of black blades inside the base of the saucer.

"Activating Extract-o-Tron with Turbine Tech, patent

pending," said Talbot, adjusting a central slider and pushing it halfway along its length.

The blades began to spin, and as the rotation increased they let out a whistle that quickly rose to a howl.

Zack's body bucked and twisted, his limbs thrown hard against the tight bonds. He let out a cry and slumped back, unconscious. His star tattoo fell dark once more.

A shaken Christopher Talbot clutched the control panel to steady himself. He sniffed the air with increasing alarm. His eyes flicked upward. The electrodes on his head sputtered with bright yellow flames. His hair was on fire. He ripped off the cap and made a move toward a fire extinguisher on the wall, but then stopped. He stood perfectly still, extended a hand, and wiggled his fingers. With a shimmy and a clank, the fire extinguisher leaped free from its bracket and flew across the room to land with a slap in his outstretched hand. It was telekinesis. Christopher Talbot began to laugh. Even as he shot a stream of foam into his own face, he continued to hoot with pleasure. "Finally!" he gloated in triumph to the camera. "I. Have. Superpowers!"

He'd done it. Christopher Talbot had successfully transferred Zack's powers into himself. But I didn't care about that. I couldn't get over the image of my brother laid out on the operating table and the sound of his agonized yell.

"We have to get to the crater. Now," I said.

The digital countdown projected onto the walls in the rest of the volcano was displayed on the computer monitors. Its glowing red numerals ran down toward zero hour. We had one hour and thirteen minutes. And counting.

I searched the computer again and this time found an icon marked "Building Systems." The elevator controls were in here, and they weren't too hard to figure out. There was a click from the darkness. And another. And then a cascade of clicking filled the still air of the laboratory, the sound receding into the shadows like an echo.

"That doesn't sound like an elevator to me," said Lara warily.

"Ah," I said, staring at the display on the screen, recognizing my error.

She folded her arms. "What did you do?"

I gave her an apologetic look, and we both turned slowly to face the banks of glass boxes arranged against the far wall. The door to each compartment lay wide open. Instead of calling the elevator I had unlocked all the cells . . . and the prisoners weren't wasting their time.

"Luke." I could hear the dread in Lara's voice. "The floor's moving."

A mass of glossy, hairy, black bodies poured from the

cases and flowed across the stone floor, chittering and hissing.

Lara's face froze in horror.

"I know why the chicken's here," she said, lifting a trembling finger to point. "Food."

A monstrous spider lumbered out of the shadows of a nightmare, a single chicken feather poking from its glistening black maw.

Without pausing, Lara unhooked her jump rope from its place on her waist, swallowed hard, and marched toward the onrushing horde. She crouched down and swished the rope, scattering them aside by the dozen. But for every squirming, scuttling collection of bodies that she cleared, another took its place. "Luke, is the elevator coming?"

"I'm working on it." My fingers flew across the keyboard as I searched the building control interface. Got to focus. Ignore the seething horde of radioactive spiders, scorpions, and ants about to sink their fangs and pincers into our soft flesh.

Heating. Nope. I switched to the next screen. *Security.* Uh-uh. Come on, elevator, where are you?

Lara's brave effort to hold off the insects was over. Ants and scorpions surged around her feet and, with a yell, she beat a hasty retreat.

I flipped to the next screen. *Transport.*

"Got it!" I shouted.

The spiders had reached the workstation. They pattered over the desk, swarmed the monitors, and clacked across the keyboard.

I felt the brush of a hairy leg as, with a trembling hand, I tapped the touchpad and called the elevator marked "Crater Level Only." I jumped up from my seat. "Lara, come on. We're leaving."

We raced toward the archway, a step ahead of the writhing black mass.

As we sped under the arch I reached down to pick up my backpack, and Lara snatched the scepter. The open elevator beckoned, and we threw ourselves inside.

There was only one button on the control panel.

"Punch it!" I yelled, and Lara smacked a palm against the chunky button.

The elevator machinery whirred as the metal doors began their painfully slow journey to come together. She mashed the button repeatedly. The gap was down to an inch when a wriggling pair of sticky spider legs forced their way between them. It was the chicken-eating monstrosity. There was the sound of scratching, and more legs speared their way inside. Lara and I pressed our backs to the compartment wall as far from the clawing legs as we could squeeze. Surely the spider wasn't strong enough to force open the doors. Was it? Just as I began to wonder if this one might have super strength, the doors closed, severing its legs. They fell to the floor and immediately curled up like paper tossed on a fire.

With a grumble of hydraulics and a whine of high-tension cable, the elevator began to rise. There was barely time to take a breath. We were heading to the crater. To Christopher Talbot. To Zack.

To save two worlds.

SECRET WEAPON

A **brightly lit** hallway led directly from the elevator to the main crater room. Halfway along it, another passage branched off to what on the official layout was labeled a daycare center, but which we strongly suspected to be a guard room. As soon as our presence was detected, reinforcements would come from there. On the ceiling the bulbous eye of a security camera swiveled to find us. I could hear the whir of its zoom lens as it homed in on our faces. They'd found us even faster than I'd hoped. No matter. We had planned for this.

I dumped my backpack at the junction, removed the plates from inside, then tipped it upside down. Sand spilled out, revealing the object I had secreted beneath. It was in two pieces, which I snapped together. I was effortlessly familiar with its design and construction, having spent countless weekends helping to build the thing.

"Is that . . . ?" Lara asked.

"Yes," I confirmed, "the plate rack. Hand me the scepter."

She passed it to me and I unscrewed the top section. It was the final part of the plate rack, which we'd cleverly disguised as an innocent Chitauri scepter.

It came together with the mechanical precision of an assassin's sniper rifle. "She doesn't look like much." I slotted the final piece into place. "But she's got it where it counts."

"She? Who calls a plate rack 'she'?"

There was a clatter of boots as Christopher Talbot's security guards pounded along the hallway. But we were ready for them. We had done our homework—not our actual homework, I mean our mission preparation—and carefully studied all of the city council plans, which included an electrical wiring map showing where all the wall sockets were located. I unspooled a power cord from the back of the plate rack and plugged it in, flicked a switch, and watched the plate rack hum to life.

This was no ordinary plate rack. When we'd started building it together my dad intended to produce something traditional, but I persuaded him we should include a few special modifications. Zack was firmly against the idea, saying it was dangerous to meddle with things we didn't understand. But he was outvoted. So the über-plate rack was born. Designed to sit on the wall above the dishwasher, it had an extending mechanical arm that plucked the freshly cleaned plates and stacked them automatically. Unfortunately, Zack had been right. The plate rack did not operate as planned. Far from it. However, if I had judged correctly, my dad's terrible DIY skills were about to hold off a frontal assault by determined security forces.

"Lock and load," I said.

Lara quickly slotted the plates we'd acquired from the buffet into the grooves on the rack. When all of them were filled, I flicked another switch and stood back.

"Fire in the hole!" I yelled.

The first of the security guards rounded the corner just as the plate rack burst into action. The extendable arm gathered a plate and, with a flick of its mechanical wrist, hurled it like a Frisbee into the lumbering pack. It caught the leading guard square in the stomach. His head flew back, knocking his plexiglass helmet off. He doubled over with an "oof" and crumpled to the floor.

I grinned at Lara. "Less a plate rack, more a fully automatic sentry gun." The plate rack was a blur, launching salvo after salvo of serving plates and saucers at the startled guards. The whistle of high-speed attack crockery split the air. As the fierce barrage held them at bay, Lara and I hurried off along the hallway. So far, so good.

The plate rack would buy us time while we gained access to the main crater room.

When we had planned our raid on the volcano, we established that the door to the crater room was secured with a state-of-the-art keyless digital lock from Home Depot. A glance at the specs told me the bad news: it was even more secure than the Kryptonyte Supalok that Zack had for his Diamondback mountain bike with twenty-inch wheels, and that was practically unbreakable.

However, there was one chink in the device's technological armor. The lock's secondary power source was a built-in battery backup. According to the very helpful man at Home Depot I had spoken to, the battery didn't kick the instant the main power was lost. It took two seconds for the lock to reboot using the internal battery. In those two seconds its defenses were down—the door would be unlocked. All we had to do was trigger a power cut throughout the entire volcano.

I dug out my cell phone and speed-dialed Lara's My Little Phoney.

"'Allo?" answered Serge.

"Are you in position?"

"*Oui*. I have located the vending machine on the fourth floor."

As well as being an expert on comics, Serge was

a whiz with vending machines. During our mission preparation we had determined that the flagship store—like the rest of Crystal Comics's stores—was fitted with the finest vending machine in the world: the Supasnax MMS Combo Fusion.

This was crucial to our plan.

Several months ago, during a particularly fierce sugar craving, Serge had ordered six chocolate bars, two bags of chips, and a can of Mountain Dew from one of these Supasnax machines all in *under thirty seconds*. The shock of the order had overwhelmed the machine's delicate internal systems, causing the Supasnax to crash, tripping the electrical circuits, plunging the store into darkness. A sweep through the vending machine repair online discussion forums revealed this to be a "known issue."

"You know what to do," I said into the phone.

"Affirmative," came back Serge's response.

"And Serge?"

"*Oui?*"

"Good luck, my friend. We're all counting on you."

"I will not let you down, *mon ami*."

"Go on my signal."

"Roger that."

Outside the door to the crater room I turned to Lara.

"When Serge cuts the power, we'll have two seconds to get inside."

She narrowed her eyes. "My middle name is 'two seconds.'" She pressed her shoulder to the door. "Now tell Serge to blow this thing!"

I lifted the phone and barked, "GO!"

"No go! I repeat, no go!" Serge's voice clamored from the handset. "We have a problem. There is no Twix. I repeat, no Twix in the Supasnax."

This was disastrous. There was just a single combination of chocolate bars and chips that would cause the vending machine to malfunction. I glanced down the hallway. The plate rack's ammunition was depleted—only a few trays remained. In less than thirty seconds the security guards would break through our last line of defense.

Although my heart was racing, I tried to keep my voice calm.

"Serge, listen to me very carefully," I said into the phone. "Tell me what you see."

I could hear Serge's shallow breathing as he ran through the list. "M&M's, Snickers, Skittles, Twizzlers, Hershey's." There was a pause. "Wait *un* moment. *Hershey's?* That is not correct. I have never seen such a chocolate bar within a Supasnax before. It is an anomaly."

"I thought he said it was a Hershey's?" puzzled Lara, who was listening in.

"I think per'aps this is the answer," said Serge with growing confidence. "The Hershey's, it has been substituted for the Twix." I heard the crack of knuckles as he faced off against the vending machine. "So, Supasnax MMS Combo Fusion," he growled, "now it is just you and *moi*."

There was the speedy clink of coins dropping through a slot and then a series of rapid-fire taps on the keypad. I'd never heard anyone select confectionery so fast.

"Luke, the plate rack's out of ammo," yelled Lara. "Here they come!"

The snarling security guards leaped over the now useless weapon. They were almost on top of us.

The hallway lights flickered, there was a whine of air-conditioning fans slowing, and we were plunged into darkness. Serge had done it!

"Lara, go!" I cried.

We had just two seconds. In the pitch black Lara shouldered her way through the unlocked door, and I hurled myself after her. Once inside we quickly heaved the door closed. The guards were hot on our tails. One of them forced a boot through the closing gap. But he was too late. The weighty door squeezed his foot like a melon in a vise, and with a shout of pain he yanked it out. The door clanged shut.

The electrical power reset itself, the overhead lights sprang back to life, and the air-conditioners began once more to pump cool air.

We'd made it inside the crater room.

But we were too late.

33

THE QUINTESSENCE

The video we'd watched had given us an impression of the crater, but only now that we were standing there did we appreciate its true scale.

It was a lot smaller than it looked on TV.

I reckoned our school gym was bigger, though not as well-equipped for world domination. Rough stone walls rose to the height of a city bus, sloping up to the perfectly flat disk of a steel roof. Light came from high-intensity spotlights set into the walls and from vertical glass tubes containing blobs of fire that mimicked lava eruptions, which were dotted across the floor like glowing exclamation points. Around the edges of the room stood metal lockers; directly above them ran some kind of monorail, and in the center squatted the doughnut-shaped control panel, made up of a ring of sleek, curved touch screens set above a series of buttons and levers.

Christopher Talbot stood with his back to us, hunched

over the controls, hands skimming across the touch screens like a pair of insects skating over a pond. Next to him my brother lay manacled to the operating table. Zack was conscious, but barely.

Something didn't make sense. Christopher Talbot appeared to be draining Zack's superpowers from him. Again. The power transfer was almost over, and the roar of the fan device filled the giant crater. It was as if we were watching the same video as the one we'd pulled up on the computer in the cavern—except for one crucial difference.

Christopher Talbot had changed his outfit. No longer in his regular suit or his biohazard gear, he wore a skin-tight blue top that showed off his muscles and clingy pants that made his thighs bulge. A dark blue cape edged in silver trim hung from his broad shoulders, and a silver mask sat high on his forehead, ready to be pulled down to complete his super costume. A sigil shone from his chest. It was similar to Zack's star tattoo, except that it looked more professional, as if he'd hired some fancy design agency to reinterpret it. I glanced down. On his feet he wore a pair of plaid slippers like my Grandpa Bernard's.

My brother twisted and writhed on the table. His lips parted to let out a shattering cry.

"Zack!" I called out to him.

"Luke?" His voice was weak.

"I'm with Lara," I said. "We're here to rescue you."

Before I had taken two steps toward him, a gang of Tal-bots converged on us from the edges of the room.

"Don't-even-think-about-it!" the leader squawked as they pressed us back toward the door.

These were not like the robots serving snacks at the party below. Their vacuum cleaner bodies were armored, and instead of trays they sported slim metal wands whose ends crackled with vicious blue sparks.

Christopher Talbot didn't seem surprised to see us. With the superpower transfer complete, he switched off the machine and removed his electrode cap. His thick hair—less thick now, more patchy and burned—smoked gently, while flames licked across his forehead. Casually he extended an arm and used his freshly acquired telekinesis to activate an extinguisher, dousing the fire.

"Luke, Laura, how nice to see you both again."

"It's Lara," said Lara tightly.

Christopher Talbot made a face as if to say, "Who cares?"

"I confess I didn't expect you to make it this far. So, bravo." He applauded, but it was a hollow, mocking sound. "However, your foolish attempt to rescue Zack is over. You failed. See that?" He lifted a hand and zipped it through the air, making a whooshing noise as he did so. "That was 'the nick of time.' And you didn't make it . . . in."

I felt my blood boil. The smart part of my brain was telling me to wait for a better opportunity, but it was being shouted down by the angry and illogical part. I balled my hands into fists at my side and started toward the smirking Christopher Talbot.

"Ah-ah." He wagged a finger and then dipped it down to point at the jostling ring of robots blocking my path. "Allow me to introduce my Assault Tal-bots."

"Assaultalbots?" Lara frowned.

"No," he grumbled. He spoke slowly, forming each syllable with immense care. "Assault. Tal-bots."

As if to underline its role as Christopher Talbot's mechanical thug, one of the robots trundled its fat, cylindrical body over my toes. I winced. It waved its crackling wand and squawked, "Ex-trapolate . . . Ex-purgate . . . Ex-cavate." The other Tal-bots joined in, screeching words beginning with "ex." Though I noted that they were all very careful not to say, "Exterminate."

"I'd stay put if I were you," warned Christopher Talbot. "One zap from that weapon will cause instant neuromuscular incapacitation." He shrugged. "Non-lethal, but *extremely* painful." He gestured toward Zack.

"As your brother will confirm. Or at least he would, if I hadn't drained him of his superpowers, leaving him a husk of his former self."

"You're a monster," spat Lara.

"On the contrary," said Christopher Talbot, offended. "I'm the hero."

"You're diluted," she said scornfully.

He looked understandably puzzled.

"Deluded," I explained.

"Oh." He nodded.

"Yeah," said Lara. "That too."

I had to agree with her. He was kidding himself if he thought he was the good guy.

"Look around you, Christopher Talbot," I said. "We're in your secret volcano headquarters, surrounded by your robot henchmen, with a genuine superhero—*whom you kidnapped*—hooked up to your superpower-sucking machine, while you put the whole world at risk. Face it, doesn't get any more villainous than that."

"That's ridiculous," he spluttered. "You have no idea what I'm *really* doing here."

"Yes, we do," I said. "We watched a video."

"Oh." He paused. "Well, good. Saves me from having to waste precious time explaining it to you. And since you so clearly understand *everything*," he said bitterly, "you'll know that I have heroic work to do and not much time to do it. So, if you'll excuse me . . ." With a snap of his cape he turned his back and started swiping at the touch screens again, muttering to himself.

I could tell that he was disappointed at not getting to make a big speech explaining his plan in detail. Classic supervillain behavior.

I had an idea. If Christopher Talbot wanted to be the hero so much, then perhaps if I proved to him he was behaving like the villain, he'd see sense and stop.

"So what's your superhero name, then?" I asked.

He spun around, bursting to tell us. "The ancients believed that there were *five* elements, not four," he began. "Earth, air, water, fire, and the stuff that stars are made of—the fifth element, the *quintessence*." He gestured to the pattern of stars on his chest. Now I could see that they vaguely formed the letter "Q." "For I am the Quintessence," he declared, putting his hands on his hips and puffing out his chest.

"Oh, come on," I said, "that's clearly a supervillain name."

"It is not," he protested. "It's classy. Enigmatic. And anyway, it's a lot better than Star Guy. I mean, what kind of name is that for a superhero anyway?"

A few weeks ago I would have agreed with him, but

the name had grown on me. Christopher Talbot returned to the control doughnut. "Besides, *you* are the ones dressed in supervillain outfits!"

"Yes, but only because it said to on your invitation," said Lara.

He prodded his chest. "I'm the only superhero. I'm the one." He sounded like a spoiled brat. I was determined to prove to him that he was the Lex Luthor of this situation.

"So," I said, picking my words as carefully as if I was laying a minefield—which I kind of was—"would you agree that now that you've neutralized us as a potential threat, there are no significant obstacles left between you and your ultimate goal?"

He nodded smugly. "As you say . . . nothing can stop me now!" A laugh burst out of him like an evil burp. With a look of horror he clamped both hands over his mouth.

"Ha!" I pointed an accusing finger. "Only the villain would say that!"

He gazed slowly around the crater room, and I could see the terrible realization dawn. He knew what he was. But plenty of villains experience a change of heart at the end of the story and turn into heroes. Would he be one of them?

"No matter," he said at last. "Once I've knocked out

Nemesis and saved the world no one will care how I got there."

There was my answer—a villain to the end.

"The world will be eternally grateful to"—he lowered his voice—"the Quintessence."

"Two worlds," I corrected him.

"How's that?"

"Star Guy was chosen to save this world and another parallel world where red is green and sponge cake tastes different. Not completely different. Just a little different."

A look of uncertainty flashed across Christopher Talbot's face. "No one said anything about saving *two* worlds."

"Well, there it is. Now, it's a big job. So you've got to ask yourself, are you up to it?"

He sniffed. "The Quintessence is up to any challenge. The bigger, the better. Two worlds? No problem." He waggled his fingers. "Bring it on."

"You're making a terrible mistake," said Lara." You have to let Star Guy fulfill his mission. He was chosen to save us from Nemesis."

"Oh, really? He's the Chosen One, is he?" Irritated, he swished his cape in Zack's direction. "Explain to me why some random kid from the suburbs should be given superpowers, hmm? Who decided that?"

"Zorbon," I said, "the Decider."

Christopher Talbot frowned. "Well, *Zorbon* clearly made a mistake. I've spent my whole life and every penny I've earned trying to turn myself into a superhero. Y'know, I could've lived like a king, bought myself an actual mansion. But a long time ago I said to myself, 'No, Chris, that's not the way.' Sacrifices had to be made. And if living in a miserable duplex and driving a ten-year-old Ford Pinto meant I could spend more on super-power research, then so be it." He reached for the control panel and snatched up what looked like an Xbox controller from its cradle. "But I have to thank your brother for something. When he bounced onto the scene as Star Guy, I realized that my dreams were within reach. If powers could be given, then they could also be *taken*."

"But you didn't have to take Zack's powers," I said. "Not every superhero needs superpowers. A lot of them train for years, honing mind and body to become crime fighters. You could have gone the Batman route."

Talbot held up his hands. "You don't think I tried?" He crossed to one of the lockers that ringed the room and pulled open the door. "Do you know how many secret orders of martial arts–practicing monks there are in the snow-capped mountains of Tibet?"

I shook my head.

"None," he said. "Not one. And I searched. Boy, did

I search. There wasn't a temple bell in that place I didn't ring."

"They do Tae Bo classes at the sports center," I suggested.

He made a face. "It's not the same." Inside the locker hung a rack of spare superhero costumes identical to the one he was wearing—capes on coat hangers, masks on the shelf above. He reached down and collected a pair of shiny black boots. "Now, I really must save the world."

"Worlds," Lara reminded him curtly.

Ignoring her, he slapped a sequence of buttons on the game controller and waggled the joystick. From the back of the room came a rumble, and then a massive shape swung out of the shadows. It was the biggest exosuit I'd ever seen. Twice as large as the one he had used to kidnap Zack, it hung from the monorail, a giant's suit on a hanger. This must have been what the plans in the basement laboratory were for.

The giant suit consisted of a hard shell with arms and legs as thick as tree trunks and was topped with a bulbous helmet with a wraparound glass visor that gleamed dully under the lights. The casing was painted in the same blue and silver colors as Christopher Talbot's clingy superhero suit. The chest was dominated by the "Q" sigil, but the bulk of the machine lay around its middle, where a ring of solid rocket boosters was slung like a bandolier of ammunition. The suit was so big there were metal handholds on the surface to help with climbing in and out. Christopher Talbot wiggled the joystick on the controller. The suit shot along the rail toward him and stopped, swaying gently. There was a click, and then the suit released from the rail and dropped to the floor with a thud, its knee joints bowing under the enormous weight before straightening. It stood like a tower.

"Behold, the Mark Fourteen Sub-Orbital Super Suit." He tucked the game controller into his belt, kicked off his slippers, and began to pull on the boots.

"Sub-orbital? Does that mean you're going to the edge of space in this thing?" I asked.

Pulling on the second boot he hopped to the control donut. "Indeed! I shall ride my white charger into battle with the dragon Nemesis."

"Does it work as well as your coatrack thing?" asked Lara with a raised eyebrow.

"Listen, I don't have to stand here answering insolent questions from the likes of you. I'm on a schedule. But for your information, Miss Smart Aleck, I will pilot the Mark Fourteen to the vicinity of the asteroid, and once in position I will save the world using my superpowers."

"*Zack's* powers," I reminded him.

I could see he didn't care about where the powers came from—they were his now. He started to list them. "The ability to breathe in outer space, telepathy for lag-free communication with planet-based authorities, radar to precisely track the asteroid's course, a forcefield to stop it—"

"—and telekinesis to push it out of the earth's path," I finished. I'd always known that Zorbon had given Zack those particular powers for a purpose, but Christopher Talbot had put it all together. I was impressed.

"Very good, Luke," he said. I could have sworn he sounded sad. "Under different circumstances I think you and I could've been friends." He thought for a moment. "Well, master and disciple." He adjusted the long stalk of a microphone.

"Commence preflight diagnostics," he commanded.

"Preflight diagnostics initiated," said the suit. It was a woman's voice. She sounded as if she was lying on a purple velvet sofa, eating grapes.

"Check superpower levels."

"Superpower levels at maximum," reported the suit. "Estimated time until empty: two hours."

"Excellent!" Christopher Talbot grinned.

"Two hours until empty?" What did that mean? At last, I understood. I knew why he'd had to extract

Zack's superpowers not once, but again. And again. "The powers—they're not stable, are they? You have to keep recharging yourself."

"A temporary state of affairs," he said dismissively. "But this is hardly like charging a cell phone—I am operating at the forefront of experimental superpower science. Which means, yes, once transferred into my body there are a few . . . stability issues. Nevertheless, it's taken me just a week"—he smoothed a hand over his hair—"a great number of fire extinguishers, and a lot of hair conditioner to get to this point. As of today a single transfer from your brother gives me up to two hours of superpowers on standby. One, if I make a tele-pathic call."

It didn't sound like much to me. "But what if you've got it wrong? What if your powers run out at the crucial moment?"

"Impossible," he snapped.

He seemed utterly certain of himself, which only made me more doubtful. All the people I'd ever met who were that sure of themselves were either bullies or gym teachers, neither of whom I would trust with the future of all mankind.

Right then I knew he couldn't succeed. Zorbon had chosen Zack for a reason. Only Star Guy had the power to stop Nemesis.

The digital countdown stood at fifty-four minutes . . .

"The truly heroic thing to do," I said, "would be to let Star Guy do his job."

"Forget about Star Guy," Christopher Talbot grumbled.

He prodded the game controller, sending commands through the air to the Mark Fourteen. The front of the suit swung open to reveal a space for a pilot that included a convenient cubbyhole for a cape.

"Preflight checks complete," purred the suit. "Ready for launch."

"Open the roof," he instructed.

There was a series of clicks and whirs. High above us the metal disk slowly began to slide back to reveal the night sky.

"Oh, and don't get any clever ideas about releasing your brother after I've gone. My Assault Tal-bots are programmed to deal harshly with any attempt to thwart my plans." Replacing the game controller in its cradle on the control donut, he strode toward the suit.

As if to reinforce their master's claim, the Tal-bots shuffled their positions, forming a solid line of evil robots between the super suit and us. They rocked back and forth, eager for a fight.

"Come-on-ugly," they taunted.

"Back off," spat Lara. "Leave him alone."

"Oooh," hooted the Tal-bots. "Is-she-your-girlfriend?

Do-you-kiss-her? I-bet-you-kiss-her. Smoochie-smoochie."

I ignored them. The roof continued to slide open. In that instant I knew that as soon as it rolled all the way back, everything would be OK.

"Luke, why are you smiling?" whispered Lara.

"He's miscalculated," I said. "Starlight is about to flood the crater and bring Zack back to full strength." I looked up expectantly. "Any moment . . . now."

"Oh, no," gasped Lara.

The roof was open, but instead of a sky full of stars all I could see were clouds.

"That wasn't the forecast," I muttered.

"It's not cloud; it's smoke," said Lara.

The gray shroud obscuring the sky wasn't a cloud bank, but smoke from all the fires we'd seen burning across the city. The dense barrier prevented starlight from reaching Zack. Without it he was powerless . . . and we were all doomed.

Christopher Talbot climbed into the Sub-Orbital Super Suit using the exterior handholds. He slid his arms and legs into its bulky frame.

I had to do something. Fast. Looking along the tightly spaced rank of Tal-bots, I had an idea. I caught Lara's attention and flicked my eyes at the jump rope coiled on her hip. She nodded in understanding and, taking a step to the side, threw one end of the rope to me. "Catch!"

I plucked the handle out of the air. Lara dived to one end of the row of Tal-bots while I scrambled to the other. The rope went taut.

"Now!" I shouted.

Together we ran forward, using our makeshift trip wire to snag the robots in the middle of their fat vacuum cleaner bodies, tipping them over. They tumbled head over heels like a row of foosball players.

"I-have-fallen-and-I-can't-get-up!" they screeched.

Unable to right themselves, the robots spun their tracks uselessly in the air. Our way was clear.

The front of the super suit clamped shut. There was a hiss of hydraulic locking bolts as Christopher Talbot sealed himself inside the pressurized suit, ready to blast off.

"Ten seconds to launch," said the suit. "Nine . . ."

With a series of beeps the super suit backed into position directly beneath the center of the crater.

I raced to Zack's side, calling to Lara, "Help me release him!" As I hurtled past the control doughnut, I snatched the game controller from its cradle and tucked it into the waistband of my pants.

"Five . . ."

Inside the super suit, Christopher Talbot lifted his arms to the sky. The super-strong alloy arms mimicked his action, rotating upward and locking in place.

"Four . . ."

"Hurry!" Frantically we unlocked the cuffs securing Zack's arms and legs and helped him to his feet. As I put one arm around his shoulder, he looked at me blearily. "Is that my phone?"

"Three . . ."

The solid rockets ignited. Jets of flame shot out of the base, blackening the crater floor.

"Luke!" yelled Lara over the roar of the engines. "What are you doing?!"

"Two . . ."

"Must get Zack to the starlight." I leaped onto the suit, dragging him behind me.

"One . . ."

Desperately I looped Zack's arms through the handholds and then did the same with my own.

"Hold on," I shouted, then closed my eyes and muttered, "and don't look down."

"Launch," said the suit.

34

THE DARKEST HOUR

The Mark Fourteen Super Suit shook as its onboard systems directed the immense power downward. The wail of the rockets was louder than any sound I'd ever heard, and I felt like I was being cooked by the tremendous heat rising up from their blast.

There was a smell of burning rubber. I opened one eye to see that the soles of my sneakers were melting. And then, with a creak of hi-tech alloy and a waggle of flight control surfaces, we were moving. The suit lurched skyward, and my head snapped back, the dizzying tang of explosive fuel invading my nostrils. I gripped the handholds for dear life. The suit rose phoenix-like on a column of flame. In seconds we would be through the smoke barrier, and my plan to energize Zack would be a success. But before we cleared the crater rim, the super suit dove sideways.

Through the gently curving visor I glimpsed Christopher Talbot's furious face. He had spotted his unwelcome passengers and was trying to shake us off. He throttled back on the rockets, deploying directional thrusters located in the suit's palms and soles to guide it on a zigzag course around the inside of the crater. We bounced around as if we were riding a wild horse.

I locked my arms through the handholds and clung on. But Zack was still dazed from having his superpowers drained. One hand fell limply away from the rung it had been clutching. The fingers of his other hand started to loosen. I shouted at him to hang on, but my voice was drowned out by the din of the thrusters. Desperately, I clawed my way across the hull. Zack was hanging on by a finger when I clasped his wrist. With a grunt I heaved his hand back into place and wrapped his fingers around the handhold.

Christopher Talbot sent the super suit on a course that veered inches from the walls and swooped impossibly low over the floor. We skimmed toward Lara, and I saw her dive into the costume locker for cover. The fiery rocket blast turned the Assault Tal-bots into slag metal. When we had passed over them, all that was left was a series of bubbling pools of silver.

But I was ready for Christopher Talbot's maneuvering

with some of my own. When we were on the ground I'd watched him use the wireless game controller to control the super suit. I had plucked it from its cradle, and it now sat securely at my waistband. I felt for the boomerang-shaped controller.

It was gone.

All the aerobatics must have dislodged it. That was it. Game over. We were finished. But then, to my surprise, the super suit steadied, settling in to a hover beneath the rim of the open roof. The howl of the engine subsided. There was a squawk of communications static, and then Christopher Talbot's voice crackled from built-in speakers.

"Luke Parker, once you've got your mind set on something, you're a difficult boy to shake."

"So my mom and dad tell me."

"But I'm onto your scheme. Hitch a ride to the stars and restore your brother's powers. Very clever. Very brave. Oh, and stupendously foolish. However, your mere presence is having an undesirable effect on my mission. My flight plan has been precisely calculated, and I hadn't factored in your additional weight. I've run the numbers through the onboard computer, and I can't make it to the Nemesis asteroid with you two playing limpet. Now, I could use my telekinetic power to scrape you off the paintwork like a couple of streaks of bird poop." He paused. "But I'd rather not waste the juice." He lowered his voice to a whisper. "And there is another way."

Something told me I shouldn't ask, but I couldn't help myself. "What's that?"

He smiled. "When you're growing up everyone tells you the same thing. 'Always be yourself.'" He pouted. "It's not a bad message, just a horrendously ordinary one. That's why I prefer comics. They ask the question 'What if you could be someone else? Someone with real power. What if you could be . . . Superman?'" He angled his head. "So, yes, always be yourself. Unless you can be Superman." His blue eyes shone through the visor, its curved glass reflecting flames from the idling rockets. He growled, "Then always be Superman."

"I don't understand."

He sighed. "I'm offering you power, Luke. *Super*power. You know I have the technology to make it happen."

The super suit bobbed in the mouth of the crater, thrusters automatically correcting its attitude to keep it level. There was a hum as one of the massive arms rotated in front of me and offered its hand. "Join me, Luke. And together we will save the world."

I glanced at Zack. Already weakened by Christopher

Talbot's experiments, he looked even more washed-out after the roller-coaster rocket ride. My whole life I'd been second best to him. Smaller, weaker, invisible. This might be my only chance to change that.

"Just look at him. It's obvious your brother was given superpowers in error. Isn't it better that they go to someone who can fully appreciate them?"

"I suppose."

"Someone who knows the only thing that Galactus is afraid of."

"The Ultimate Nullifier," I mouthed.

"Someone who knows who'd win in a race between Superman and the Flash."

"The Flash. But only since 1970."

"Someone like you."

I thought about my brother and our last real conversation, on the night of his kidnapping. "Zack said that Zorbon the Decider picked the wrong brother. He was unhappy and wished he hadn't been given superpowers. So, in a way, I'd be doing him a favor."

"Exactly!" Christopher Talbot leaped on the notion.

"And it's not as if I'd be doing anything evil."

"*No-o-o-o.*"

"After all, you're not interested in taking over the world. You only want to save it, right?"

"I'm all about the saving."

I bit my lip. "I don't know . . ."

"Oh come on, Luke. *Lukester.* It's time to make up your mind. So, what's it to be—are you with me?"

Was I? You'd think that years of reading comics in which superheroes do the right thing—sacrifice themselves for the greater good, see through the villain's deception—would have prepared me for this moment. But I'd be lying if I said I wasn't tempted. You can't blame me. If someone offered you your wildest dream, what would you do? Come on, I was eleven. I needed a sign.

And then it happened. Not a gravelly voice telling me to use the Force. Or a S.H.I.E.L.D. directive winging its way to me on encrypted frequencies. No. It was a feeling.

And it was coming from my underpants.

A gentle vibration told me immediately what had happened. The game controller had slipped past the waistband of my pants, but caught on the elastic of my Daredevil undies. My second-luckiest pair.

I needed to buy time while I rummaged.

"Would I get to wear a cape?" I asked.

Christopher Talbot sighed. "Any color you want."

"And a mask?"

"Naturally. Now, just let me deal with this little space rock problem, and then we'll get you fitted out with a bespoke costume and, of course, those lovely superpowers. It'll be great. You can be my sidekick."

My fingers closed around the solid shape of the game controller.

"I don't think so," I said, drawing it out.

"What?!" Talbot choked as he saw what I was holding. "You can't. Luke, I thought we had an understanding. Don't do this." Inside I could see him frantically working the onboard controls. But he was too late.

I braced myself against the hull and thumbed the FIRE button.

"NO!" he shrieked.

The main engines detonated, and in the space of a heartbeat we cleared the crater rim. The volcano disappeared beneath us like a coin dropped down a deep well. In the next second the speeding super suit entered the dense band of smoke. My eyes were stinging, and briefly I lost sight of Zack. For what felt like an eternity, I was alone in the gray nothing.

In that moment I found my mind hurtling back to a long time ago. When I was very little, my mom and dad projected a light show on the ceiling above my crib to help me nod off to sleep. I don't actually remember it, since I was too young, but I know about it because there's a photograph of me taken at the time. In the photo I'm fast asleep, clutching my cuddly rabbit, tucked under my Jedi blanket—and above me, the ceiling twinkles. With stars.

We broke through the smoke barrier. The night sky opened up before us. Nine thousand one hundred and ten stars shone their light down on Zack.

Our rapid passage through the air sent up little whirlwinds of turbulence on the outer edges of the suit, which continued to climb at an alarming rate. Ferocious winds whipped at my face. My hands felt numb. I knew I couldn't hold on much longer.

The stars on Zack's chest began to glow faintly and then with more vigor. His strength was returning.

"Where . . . where am I?" His words were snatched out of his mouth by the relentless gale. He looked down and let out a cry, then caught sight of me clinging to the hull of the super suit. "Luke?" I heard his voice in my head. He was using telepathy. At least one power was back.

"What are you doing here?" he asked.

"Trying to rescue you."

"Well, you're not doing a very good job."

He was so annoying.

But he was also our only hope. Zorbon the Decider had given Zack six powers to defeat Nemesis. Five of them had already revealed themselves. It was now or never for number six. The final power. The one I had been waiting for since that night in the tree house. Who was I kidding? I'd been waiting for this one since my dad used to zoom me around the yard when I was a toddler. I just had a feeling.

I let go.

"Luke!" cried Zack, reaching uselessly for me as I fell past him.

He swiped at thin air.

I fell through the darkness. A skydiver free-falls at about a hundred and twenty miles an hour. A peregrine falcon dives on its prey at a speed of two hundred miles an hour. They know what they're doing. I began to spin uncontrollably. My stomach felt as if it was trying to burst out through my mouth; my eyeballs bulged in their sockets as the g-force tore at my body. The edges of my vision started to dim. But just before I blacked out I caught sight of something above me. Closing in fast. A streak of light in the darkness.

Like a shooting star.

A second later I felt arms grasp me, and I was no longer falling.

"Got you!" said Zack's voice in my head.

My stomach and eyeballs returned to their usual positions.

"I knew it!" I trumpeted in my head. "I knew it!"

Then I had an awful thought. I looked down and then at Zack. "You *are* flying, right? We're not both just plummeting to our certain deaths, are we?"

"I *am* flying," reassured Zack.

"Oh, good, that's a relief."

Above us I could see the red glow of engines from the Mark Fourteen Super Suit as it burned sharply toward the edge of the atmosphere and its rendezvous with Nemesis. Whatever I thought of his methods, I had a sneaking admiration for Christopher Talbot's stubborn determination.

The vast asteroid blazed its own determined course, but the weird thing was that from here it appeared to be stationary. In truth it was already between the moon and the earth, closing the distance between us at a speed of some twenty-seven thousand miles an hour. It hung over the horizon, a gray-black disk of nothingness ready to swallow everything and everyone I had ever known. Lara and Serge. My mom and dad, my grandparents. Every one of us teetered on the edge of a bottomless hole, and if we tumbled in, we would fall forever. Only one thing stood between us and total destruction. And it wasn't Christopher Talbot.

"Zack. Nemesis is coming."

"I know. But first we have to get you back on the ground."

"How fast can you fly?"

"No idea." He grinned. "Let's find out. Now, hold tight."

"I am not cuddling you."

"Oh, for—Just hang on, will you?"

We dove earthward, back toward home and the comic book store. In less than a minute we had spotted the volcano. Zack circled the open crater once and then dropped down. We landed heavily, and he spilled me onto the floor.

"Sorry," he said.

But I forgave him, since it was his first landing. I struggled to my feet, brushing myself off.

"Luke, you're alive!" Lara hurled herself on top of me, almost knocking me back over. "When you took off like that I was sure you were toast."

"*Mon ami!*"

It was Serge. He too began to hug me. Then he turned to stand in awe of my brother. "It is you."

"Hi, Serge," said Zack.

"He knows my name."

I sighed. "Of course he knows your name. It's Zack; he's known you for years." There wasn't time for any of this fanboy nonsense. I crossed to the costume locker, pulled out a cape and mask, and thrust them at my brother. "Here, put these on."

"We've been through this," he complained. "I'm not wearing that stuff."

"The mask isn't to protect your identity; it's the rest of us I'm worried about. You might want fame, but speaking as your brother, I'd prefer not to have a camera shoved in my face every time I leave the house."

"OK, OK," he relented, "I'll wear the mask." Reluctantly, he looped it over his head. "But not the cape."

I didn't have a good reason for the cape. I just really, really wanted him to wear one.

"My sister Cara has a thing for capes," said Lara.

"She does?" Zack swallowed. "A thing. When you say 'a thing,' what kind of . . . ? Y'know what? Doesn't matter right now. Gimme the cape." He grabbed it out of my hands and flung it over his shoulders.

Serge pointed at the monitors on the control doughnut. "The nuclear missiles, they are launching!" The countdown was running out, and TV pictures from around the world showed nuclear silos opening and missiles moving into their firing positions. Four minutes and counting.

We all looked at Zack. Somehow, what had started with an unfortunately timed pee and an unpronounceable visitor from a parallel world, had led inescapably to this moment. I wanted to say something. Something meaningful, something supportive. After all, it might be the last thing anyone ever said to him.

"Zack," I said, "don't mess it up."

He smiled, then tilted his face up to the night sky framed by the crater rim. He steeled himself, bent his knees, and then sprang into the air. We watched him soar through the open roof, cape billowing out behind him like a ripple in space-time, silver mask shining, chest pulsing with starlight. The smoke had thinned, which meant we were able to follow his arrow-straight progress. He hurled his tiny body into the void, a speck against the monstrous Nemesis. Beside me, Serge began to mutter.

"Granted cosmic superpower
In our darkest hour,
Star Guy, star light,
Protector of the world tonight."

Somehow, this time, it didn't seem so cheesy.

35

THE COSMIC PUNCH

Everyone on the planet knows what happened next.

On every street corner, in every café, school, and office, it was the only story on people's lips for weeks and months afterward. Cameras on the International Space Station and a bunch of military satellites captured most of the action.

In the footage you can see Star Guy racing toward Nemesis. He's caught between the asteroid in front of him and ten thousand nuclear missiles rising from the earth's surface below. On the soundtrack you can hear military chatter about vectors and threat levels and defense conditions. Star Guy uses his telepathic power to raise Earth Defense Command. When they realize he's up there, they try to abort Spitting Umbrella, but it's such a huge bombardment, and since the weapons have been fired from all over the world, it's impossible to coordinate. Only a few are deactivated in time. That leaves about eight thousand nuclear missiles spearing into the sky heading for the asteroid—and my brother.

Nemesis is now right on the edge of the earth's atmosphere. So close that even with the naked eye you can see the craters on its vast surface, and though you know it can't be true you think you can hear the asteroid howling like a wild animal.

Star Guy uses his radar to lock on to all of the remaining warheads, then forms his force field into a cone shape, so that when the missiles strike it they are pushed out and around the asteroid, shooting off into space to explode harmlessly.

The missiles taken care of, he's about to turn his attention to Nemesis when *WHAM!* The Mark Fourteen Super Suit slams into him, knocking him unconscious. In all the commotion no one has noticed Christopher Talbot creeping up through the atmosphere, presuming that the blip on the radar was just another missile.

So now Star Guy's just floating there limply, while in his super suit Christopher Talbot moves into position, extending his giant mechanical arms, directing his own telekinetic power at the asteroid. It quickly becomes obvious that nothing is happening. He's run out of superpower.

He jiggles his arms, as if he can shake out the last ounce, but it's gone. He's no superhero, just an ordinary, foolish man hovering before a planet-killing asteroid. A second later he's struck by a flaming chunk of rock, which sends him spinning off toward the dawn horizon. Neither the super suit nor Talbot's body was ever found, and to this day no one knows what happened to him.

Meanwhile, Star Guy is floating like a piece of space junk. In my head I'm screaming at him to wake up. Since then, I discovered that everyone I talk to was doing the same thing at exactly the same time. Zack's never been good at getting up in the morning, especially since becoming a teenager, but all of that telepathic shouting must have been too hard to ignore. Star Guy's eyes flicker. He's back in business.

With a kick of his legs he flies straight at the asteroid and, raising his arms into position above his head, he summons every drop of his telekinetic powers. He looks a bit like the Titan Atlas who held up the earth's sphere. (You've probably seen his statues.) Flames start to shoot from Star Guy's heels as he skids against the upper atmosphere, pushed back by Nemesis's seemingly unstoppable force.

Suddenly, one of the military operators at Earth Defense Command squawks, "We are seeing a course correction for Nemesis. I repeat. The asteroid just changed direction!"

But then they do the calculations, and it's not

enough. Nemesis has only shifted its path by a degree, which means it won't miss the earth. And then things turn really bad.

A split opens up in space. As Zorbon the Decider predicted, the asteroid is actually tearing the fabric of space-time that separates our two universes. You can see Zorbon's world through the gap. And like the wake of a boat, the passage of the asteroid is pulling the planet through into our universe—which can't be good. Nemesis is seconds away from causing transdimensional carnage. The end of the worlds is nigh.

"Star Guy," says Captain Kit Rivers of Earth Defense Command—in what will turn out to be one of the most famous phrases to come out of the whole saga. "Gotta give it the full cosmic punch, kid."

Leaving aside the fact that technically Star Guy does not have a "cosmic punch," the next part is really thrilling. In a wholly unexpected development, the starlight from Zorbon's universe shines through the tear. That, plus the light from our universe, has some sort of supercharging effect on Star Guy. Scientists have been feverishly speculating on the nature of this event ever since. In my view it's as if both universes were banding together to help him succeed. But the important thing is that, thanks to the refill, Star Guy is at the peak of his power. Blistering with the energy of a gazillion stars, he winds up to deliver his final awe-inspiring telekinetic blast and, blah blah blah, he saves the world and all of humanity and the other world too and the dolphins and the rain forests and . . . and . . . and . . .

But you know all this. You've read the reports, watched the interviews. You've probably even seen the made-for-TV movie they rushed out to mark "Yay, We're Alive!" Day. In the movie Star Guy is played by a much older actor, he has a chin like Mount Rushmore—oh, and I'm not even in it. Instead they've given Star Guy a dog. Star Pup. I mean, honestly.

The thing you don't know is what happened afterward. By the time Zack returned from the edge of space, dawn was coming. It was time to go home. Before we left the crater room, I made sure to wipe Christopher Talbot's hard drives of any evidence that would link Zack with Star Guy, and we dismantled what little the rocket blast had left of the superpower-sucking equipment. When we finally emerged from the volcano it was early morning.

Low sunlight slanted across the streets, and a freshening wind ruffled the trees in the park. The fires that had burned the previous night and caused us so much trouble were still smoldering, but apart from that the world seemed strangely ordinary. People were up and about; the buses were running. We caught the 55 home. I sat next to Lara, while behind us Serge spent the journey staring, open mouthed, at Zack, who was snoring quietly in the seat beside him.

I had taken a spare superhero costume from the locker in the crater, figuring that it would be useful in the future when one was in the laundry. As I tucked it into my backpack I saw something rolling around at the bottom. It must have been lodged there for a year.

I dug it out and offered it to Lara. "I think this belongs to you," I said. She eyed the object clutched between my fingers. It was her uni-ball Gelstick Pen with a 0.4 mm tip.

She reached for it but then stopped, and after a long time said, "Keep it." She shrugged. "I don't need it."

Lara decided not to write her story exposing Star Guy's true identity. She could have become the most famous reporter in the world, but when I asked her why she chose not to tell, she gave another of those shrugs and said there were more important things in life. Girls—mysterious and surprising.

We hung out together the rest of the summer, but before you go jumping to conclusions, there was no canoodling. We spent most of the time in the tree house, just talking and reading. And not just comics. I still read them, of course, but I like other things now too. I'm currently going through a Charles Dickens phase. Serge assures me it will pass.

The summer was flying by in a blur, and soon it would

be time to start at my new school. I was moving up to the big league. Even after everything I'd faced, I still felt scared. But *something* told me it'd all be OK. That something was my mom. She just wouldn't stop hugging me and saying, "You'll be OK."

I don't think I can fully express how happy Mom and Dad were to see Zack and me that morning. When they came down and found us in the kitchen—Zack at the table starting on his third bowl of Cheerios, me rummaging in the cupboard complaining that someone had eaten the Cocoa Puffs from my Variety Pack—you've never seen two grown-ups cry like they did. They didn't even notice when I poured myself a cup of black coffee. And the noises coming out of them! Sniveling, wailing, hiccupping sobs. Honestly, it was like being in the doctor's waiting room during a flu epidemic. But I didn't mind. I think I must be getting sappy in my old age.

On the walk back from the bus stop Zack and I had hatched a cover story to explain his reappearance, but we didn't have to use it. All Mom and Dad cared about was that he was home, we were together, and the sun had come up. They hadn't believed me that time I told them Zack was Star Guy, and they didn't bring it up again. The only awkward question we had to deal with arose a few weeks later when Dad went looking for his plate rack.

One last thing about the bus ride. Just after we

dropped off Serge, Zack stirred briefly from his well-deserved snooze to mumble something before lapsing back into sleep. Lara didn't catch it, and I said I didn't either, but that was a lie. I'm not sure why I didn't want to tell her. I turned away to stare out of the window and saw my own reflection. There was a small smile on my face.

What Zack had said was, "Luke . . . couldn't have done it without you."

And then there had been a lot more snoring.

It was two months after Zack had prevented cosmic catastrophe. We were sitting in the tree house together. I watched the last rays of the sun retreat across the dusty floor and listened to the susurration of the wind in the leaves. "Susurration" is my word of the day. It means "rustling." I have a lot more new words since I widened my reading material. That evening I was almost at the end of *Oliver Twist*. Now, there's someone whose story would've turned out a whole heap differently if he'd had superpowers.

Zack had his head in a math textbook. He'd just returned from seeing Cara. No, it's not what you think. She's still going out with Matthias the Viking. Zack's relationship with Cara is strictly professional—he's helping her prepare for physics. Every Tuesday night he trudges over there and sits with her at the kitchen table for an hour, explaining things like diffraction and Boyle's Law, when what he really wants to be explaining is how much he likes her. It's painful. When he comes home afterward he's a complete wreck. Thankfully, the rest of his life isn't as tense. Now that he can fly, he's been much better at managing his superhero/homework balance. Being able to zoom off, foil a bank raid, and be back in time for dinner has removed a lot of the pressure.

"I need to pee."

"Then go," said Zack without looking up from his textbook.

Following his poor results earlier that year he wasn't taking any chances. Tonight's study session was part of an intensive plan to prepare for finals, even though school had just begun. I know. If he hadn't saved the world, it'd be off-putting.

I clambered down the rope ladder and headed for the house. Above the old oak tree the sky was striped with dazzling oranges and yellows, feathered with white like the wings of a giant bird that could easily bite your head off in one gulp. Nemesis had left a lot of dust in the atmosphere, and everyone agreed that while our narrow scrape with extinction had been terrifying, the sunsets were spectacular.

As I crossed the yard an uneasy feeling crept up on me. Something strange was in the air, and it wasn't just asteroid dust. Could it be Zorbon the Decider? What if he chose this exact moment to return? I had been expecting him for some time. After all, he had given Zack powers in order to defeat Nemesis, but that mission was over and out. I wondered if the representative of the High Council of Frodax Wonthreen Rrr'n'fargh would return in order to remove Zack's powers.

A little over two months ago, I might have been pleased to find him stripped of his superpowers, but not now. I'd even stopped making my list of Zack's irritating points. The truth was I liked having a brother with a cool secret superhero identity. The alternative was Math Guy, and that didn't bear thinking about. Of course I'd prefer if it was me who had the superpowers, but if I really can't have them, then I'm glad it's Zack who does. And in the end, I'd rather be living in a one-superhero household than a no-superhero household.

I peed, and as I reached for the flush handle, I heard a distinctive sound.

Bloop-whoosh!

Without pausing to wash my hands, I bolted out of the house. I reached the foot of the rope ladder in time to see the flick of a purple-and-gold cape disappearing inside a blue oval transdimensional craft. A second later there was another *bloop-whoosh*—and the craft was gone. Zorbon the Decider had returned. And I'd missed him.

Again.

I found Zack sitting silently in the darkening tree house, surrounded by shadows. He'd put aside his math book. In front of him lay a sponge cake.

"It's from Zorbon," he said, biting into a slice. "It tastes different," he mused. "But not entirely different."

I didn't care about the stupid sponge cake. I had to know. "Did Zorbon take away your powers?"

He took another bite. "Um, no. But you'll never guess what did happen."

Gah! He's so annoying. "So, tell me!"

He glanced over his shoulder. From out of the shadows stepped a familiar figure. It was Lara. She wore an expression of pure astonishment. I hadn't seen anything like it since . . . oh, no.

Surely not.

"Luke," she said, staring at her hands, turning them over and over, "I think I have superpowers."

ACKNOWLEDGMENTS

Ideally, these acknowledgments would be zooming out of the page at you in massive 3-D titles, accompanied by a stirring orchestral score. Budgetary constraints, however, mean that instead I have this list. Also, I shall hum. Thanks to my editor Kendra Levin, publisher Ken Wright, and the rest of the team at Viking Children's Books; illustrator Stephen Gilpin and designer Eileen Savage for a cover as impactful as Giant-Sized X-Men Number 1; Agent Stan (literary, not S.H.I.E.L.D., sadly) for his cool-headed guidance. As ever, thanks to my wife, Natasha, who puts the dynamic in our duo. Above all, this story is for my son, Luke. I know you won't be able to read it for quite a few years, but when you're old enough to understand, the answer is no, you can't borrow the car.

DAVID SOLOMONS has been writing screenplays for many years. His first feature film was an adaptation of *Five Children and It* (starring Kenneth Branagh and Eddie Izzard, with gala screenings at the Toronto and Tribeca Film Festivals). His latest film is a romantic comedy set in the world of publishing, *Not Another Happy Ending* (Karen Gillan, Iain De Caestecker), which closed the Edinburgh International Film Festival. *My Brother Is a Superhero* is his first novel for children. He was born in Glasgow and now lives in Dorset with his wife, novelist Natasha Solomons, and their son, Luke.